"I'm not marrying you, Gray. And that's final."

"Final." Gray took a few measured steps to think that over. "Final, as in for now? Or final, as in for a few more months?"

Emma's fingers clenched around her bouquet. "Final, as in forever. Final as it gets. Final as in I'm *not* going to marry you. Not ever."

Gray shook his head. "So you're saying you probably won't marry me," he provoked a bit more. "Is that it?"

Marriages made in moments!

Finding the perfect partner isn't easy....
Enter the Cupid Committee! Quietly, secretly,
but very successfully, this group of anonymous
romantics has set hundreds of unsuspecting
singles on the path to matrimony....

Take Tess, Emma and Raine. Three best friends
who made a pact: if they're still single when they
turn thirty, they have permission to play matchmaker
for each other! But they have no idea that Cupid is
about to deliver a lightning strike....

Three women, three unexpected romances in:

August 2001: *The Provocative Proposal* (#3663)
September 2002: *The Whirlwind Wedding* (#3716)
November 2002: *The Baby Bombshell* (#3723)

DAY LECLAIRE
The Whirlwind Wedding

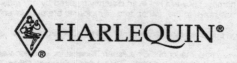

TORONTO • NEW YORK • LONDON
AMSTERDAM • PARIS • SYDNEY • HAMBURG
STOCKHOLM • ATHENS • TOKYO • MILAN • MADRID
PRAGUE • WARSAW • BUDAPEST • AUCKLAND

To Antonio Ruiz and his miracle workers,
with all my love and thanks

ISBN 0-373-03716-3

THE WHIRLWIND WEDDING

First North American Publication 2002.

Visit us at www.eHarlequin.com

Printed in U.S.A.

PROLOGUE

Seattle, Washington

"YOU may address the committee."

Grayson Shaw stepped into the splash of light that broke the darkness of the room. He lifted a hand to shade his eyes and focused in on one of the half dozen silhouettes seated behind a long conference table. "Is that you, Shadoe?"

A rough sigh emitted from the darkness. "You're not supposed to use our names." The voice grated, the tone dark and gruff. "Don't you get it? This is a *secret* committee."

Gray shrugged. "Since Shadoe isn't your real name, your anonymity is protected," he argued logically. "Now if I'd called you Tom Smith instead of using your middle name—"

"Dammit, Gray!"

"—then you'd have cause to be ticked off. But since this is some sort of matchmaking committee and not an organization intent on overthrowing the government or inciting political turmoil, I don't see the need for secrecy." He paused a beat. "Do you, Adelaide?"

Another sigh emitted from the darkness, this one from Shadoe's mother, and the head of the Cupid Committee. "Apparently not."

"Considering you're coming here to ask for our

help, you might consider following our rules,'' Shadoe complained.

"I prefer making my own rules."

"We've noticed. How did you find out about us, anyway?"

Gray folded his arms across his chest and shook his head. "That would be telling."

"It was Shayde, wasn't it? Ever since we matched him with Tess, he's lost every ounce of reason. Assuming he ever had any."

Gray suppressed a grin. That sounded like a brother talking. "He's in love."

"If that's what love does to you, I don't want any part of it." Shadoe shoved back his chair and stood. "Maybe we should disband the committee. And maybe we should do it before we cause any further disintegration in the intelligence of the male of the species."

Gray's mouth twisted in an ironic smile. "Too late, I'm afraid. At least, it's too late in my case."

"Poor bastard," Shadoe muttered.

"Stop it, Tom."

Adelaide spoke in an undertone to the remaining members of the committee. As one they stood and exited through a door at the back of the room. Crossing to a nearby panel, she flipped a switch. Light flooded down from the ceiling revealing a stark, utilitarian conference area, stripped of all but a table, a half dozen leather chairs, and a pile of nondescript folders.

"That's better, don't you think?" she asked. "All this cloak-and-dagger nonsense can be amusing, but since Gray knows who we are, it's a bit pointless."

"It still begs the same question," Shadoe retorted. "Who told you about us?"

Gray shook his head. "You should know me better

than that. You can guess all you want, but the bottom line is… I know the committee exists, and I want your help.''

"It's Emma Palmer, isn't it?'' Adelaide didn't wait for Gray to confirm the obvious. "I assume you want us to arrange a match between the two of you.''

Why did he feel as if he'd need his most formidable negotiation skills to pull this off? Foolishly he'd assumed he'd walk in and within minutes of his stating his request, the Cupid Committee would promise a match and he'd be wed by nightfall. The fact that he was dead wrong suggested the disintegration in his intelligence was occurring at a far more rapid rate than he'd anticipated.

Not that his intellectual deterioration changed anything. There was only one thing that mattered to him. *Emma Palmer.* He wanted her. Hell, if he were honest about it, he'd admit he needed her. For one brief shining moment in his life, he'd had the dream. And then he'd lost it. His mouth tightened. It didn't matter what they demanded of him or what sacrifices were required. He'd do whatever it took to have her back in his life.

His eyes narrowed in consideration as he studied Adelaide and Shadoe. Thoughts of Emma distracted him and he deliberately shoved them to one side. If he wanted to succeed, he needed to focus his attention on the problem at hand. Before he left, he'd find a way to gain the committee's cooperation. It was merely a question of how.

"Are you refusing to help me?'' Gray asked. He used the question as a throwaway in order to give himself time to marshal his counter arguments.

Adelaide hesitated. "We're willing to consider the request. But I can't promise anything.''

At least it wasn't a flat-out refusal. Time to narrow down their objections. "Are you hesitating because you don't think we're a good match? Or is it because you have other matches which take priority?"

"Neither." Shadoe responded this time. "Sometimes we turn down a request because we feel we shouldn't interfere."

Adelaide nodded. "We've discovered there are times when it's best to let nature take its course."

Gray couldn't think of anything to counter that particular objection, so he tried a different tack. "Your matchmaking skills worked with Tess and Shayde."

"Shayde didn't know what we were up to," Adelaide retorted. "Neither did Tess. It usually works best that way."

A cold knot clenched in Gray's gut as he struggled to summon a reply. Where had his negotiation skills gone? He was usually able to find a loophole to any and all arguments. But for some reason, he couldn't pull it off this time. Dammit! When it mattered most, he screwed up. "Are you saying you won't help me?" he repeated out of sheer desperation.

"Not necessarily. First, let me ask you this." She approached, fixing him with a level gaze. "Why do you need our help? Why can't you win her on your own?"

The question hit a sore spot. Because of his background, he'd always been a man who valued his privacy. He'd also prided himself on managing his own affairs whether on the business front or in his personal life. Asking for help stuck in his craw. Having people interfere stuck there even more.

Okay, fine. He could deal with that sort of discomfort. But not being in control of his own destiny, not

being able to find a way out of this particular predic-
ament, nearly sent him over the edge. If it were anyone
other than Emma he'd never—*never*—have considered
this course of action.

He clamped his back teeth together. But it *was*
Emma. She'd been the one bright spot in his life, starting when they were little more than children. She'd
been a breath of spring air in his barren, winterlike life.
Where he craved order, she created chaos. Where he
saw left or right or straight ahead, she saw up, down
and diagonal. Where he analyzed his choices between
two alternatives, she explored infinite possibilities. And
where he shied from the emotions that had created such
turmoil in his young life, she embraced them. Hell, she
was emotion in its purest, most raw form. Instead of
making the smart choice and avoiding the emotional
turmoil she stirred, he sought it out. With her, he felt
alive, something he hadn't been in more years than he
could count.

"I need your help because Emma and I haven't been
connecting recently," he admitted. Now there was an
understatement to end all understatements.

"Let me guess… From what I've learned of Emma,
she wants to go left and you want to go right."

Adelaide's comment echoed his own thoughts so
closely that a smile eased Gray's mouth. "I'd say that
about sums it up."

"So, next time she wants to go left, go with her."

Gray pretended to shudder. "If you knew Emma as
well as I did, you wouldn't suggest such a thing."

"That bad?"

"Worse."

"Then why do you want her?"

"Simple," Gray replied quietly. "I love her. I have

since she was the size of a gnat and her life revolved around how fast she could climb out of her diapers.''

Adelaide glanced at her son before nodding. "Okay, Gray. We'll see what we can do. But I should warn you about one small problem you'll face before this is over."

"What's that?"

"You're going to regret asking us to interfere. You're going to wish you'd won her on your own."

"Not a chance. I tried that avenue already and it didn't lead anywhere." He held out his hand first to Adelaide, then to Shadoe. "Thanks for your help. Let me know what you want from me and it's yours."

"We'll be sure to do that."

He hesitated. "Oh, and one last thing."

Adelaide lifted an eyebrow. "Matching you with Emma isn't enough?"

Gray shrugged. "It's a small matter, well within your abilities."

"What do you want, Shaw?" Shadoe demanded.

"Keep me apprised of your progress." It was supposed to come out as a request. Too bad it sounded more like an order. "I want to know what you're doing at all times."

"I'm sorry. We don't keep our clients in the loop," Adelaide replied. "It risks influencing the outcome in a negative manner. And that would defeat the whole purpose of our organization, wouldn't you agree?"

Gray shook his head. He couldn't accept that. He wouldn't. "Make an exception. I know you update committee members through regular e-mail correspondence. Copy me when you send out the reports. I promise I won't interfere in your plans." Logic came to his rescue. "Why would I? I want this match to work."

"I'm going to kill Shayde when I get my hands on him," Shadoe muttered. "Clients aren't supposed to know how we operate."

"But I do know." Gray frowned. He refused to smooth talk the Smiths into anything. He wasn't a con artist. Ruthless, sure. But never a con. It wasn't his style. Still, politeness couldn't be called a snow job, right? "Please. This is important."

Shadoe inclined his head. "I'll think about it."

"Thanks. I appreciate that." Gray didn't waste energy on pointless small talk. He'd accomplished what he'd come for. He'd also pushed his luck as far as Adelaide and Shadoe were concerned. If he were smart, he'd head back to San Francisco before they had a chance to reconsider. With a final nod, he turned and left the room.

The minute the door closed behind him, Adelaide sank into the nearest chair. "This isn't good. Not good at all."

"You really think he's going to be sorry he approached us?" Shadoe asked.

"Without question."

"Why?"

"Because he'll never be sure," she said in a tired voice. "He'll always wonder if his wife married him because she loves him or because we tricked her into it. And that won't sit well with a man like Gray."

Shadoe shrugged. "He approached us. We didn't go after him."

"No, but he wasn't the only one who approached us, was he?" She glanced up at him. "Emma's best friend, Tess, approached us about finding matches for her two friends months ago. If matching Tess with your brother hadn't taken precedence, we'd have dealt with this situation by now. How many requests are we up to now? Three?''

"Four, total. And every last one of them is for the same thing—get Gray and Emma together. They can't all be wrong, can they?''

"You wouldn't think so." She drummed her fingertips on the conference table. "But I suspect this match will turn out to be trickier than I'd anticipated."

"You don't think we'll fail?" Shadoe asked in disbelief. "We've never failed before."

She waved that aside. "You know perfectly well there's a first time for everything. Even something as unlikely as failure."

"Not a chance. We've had—what?—three hundred and twenty-three successful matches without a single mistake. That puts us ahead of those Cinderella Ball people, doesn't it?''

"Only by a single match. And that won't mean much if this one doesn't work out."

"It'll work out. I guarantee it."

"If only I could think of a way—" Adelaide stilled, then glanced at her son with a wide grin.

Shadoe groaned. "I know that expression, boss lady, and it invariably means trouble."

"In spades," she confirmed. "I have a plan, but if we're going to pull it off, I'll need my best man playing the part of the Instigator."

He smiled wryly. "I assume that's me?"

Warmth gleamed in her dark eyes. "Yes, sweetheart. That's you."

"Lucky me, getting to instigate the one match you think has the least chance of success."

"We can't all have the fun jobs. In fact, this plan's so crazy it might actually work." She leaned closer, her voice dropping to a whisper. "Now here's what I want you to do...."

CHAPTER ONE

Subject: Emma Palmer, Matchmaking Update
To: Committee@CupidCommittee.com
From: Shadoe@CupidCommittee.com
CC: "Mr.Trouble" <Grayson_Shaw@galaxies.net>

A reminder to all members: Saturday's report will be a day late and I better not hear any complaints about it. You want the most up-to-date information on Emma, don't you? Then quit your bellyaching. I'll e-mail all of you the first chance I get.

Emma will be off to Tess Lonigan's wedding Saturday morning. Tess was our last match, for those of you with impaired memories, and is about to marry my younger brother and fellow Instigator, Shayde. Hey, Seth! I hope you get this before you leave for the wedding. I got some interesting poop on your soon-to-be-wed sister. I bet she never told you this story. Ready for a laugh? Apparently she and Raine Featherstone (our next match), used to stay in Palmersville with Emma during college vacation. During one of those visits, Emma bet Tess that she couldn't go skinny-dipping in Nugget Creek without getting caught. The local Peeping Tom, a fellow by the name of Billy Sheraton, did his best, but Raine sicced a cat on him. (And before you start ringing my cell phone, no, I haven't found out how Raine got the cat to obey her. People around Palmersville refer to it as Raine's "gift." So, don't bother me with questions I can't answer. Or better yet, bug Gray about it. He has a knack for getting insider info.)

Emma's schedule is as follows: She makes the hour drive to San Francisco bright and early Saturday morning for a quick flight to Seattle. Then she'll be checking into the King's Crown. (FYI, that's the fancy new hotel we've been watching go up for the past couple of years.) As soon as Emma arrives she'll be attending the dress rehearsal. After that's out of the way, Tess told me the three of them intend to spend the hours leading up to the wedding wallowing in the lap of luxury "enjoying" typical female tortures—a full-body massage, a manicure and pedicure, a facial and a hair appointment. The wedding's scheduled for seven Saturday evening, and if Seth or Adelaide doesn't get to it first, I'll fill you in on all the wedding details as soon as I find a free minute. Considering that half of the Cupid Committee is either in the wedding or attending it, the rest of you can just suffer until we feel like reporting in.

Step one of the boss lady's plan is in place. Nothing should go wrong. (And no, Gray, I'm not telling you what that plan is.)

Oh, and in response to recent inquiries.... Grayson Shaw is definitely scheduled to attend the ceremony. Rumor has it he'll be escorting Emma down the aisle. Or is it up? Whichever, it'll give all of those attending the ceremony the opportunity to assess the situation. (Right, Gray?)

Shadoe, Cupid Committee Instigator Extraordinaire Reporting from Palmersville, California (while attempting to keep a low profile)

SO MAYBE this wasn't the worst day of her life. Though as bad days went, this one ranked right up there as top ten in horrendous. Emma Palmer double-checked the room number on the slip of paper she held and then compared it to the number on the door. It matched. All she had to do was knock. Simple, right? She grimaced. Not so simple, mainly because she didn't want to talk to the man on the other side of the door.

It was bad enough that she'd missed her best friend's dress rehearsal due to her flight developing last-minute mechanical problems. But she'd also missed all the fun things she, Tess and Raine had planned for the hours leading up to the wedding ceremony. Top that off with lost luggage, the hotel giving her room away and now a last-minute chore her grandfather had requested. At this rate, she'd never get to the church and Tess would never forgive her.

Well, the sooner she knocked, the sooner she'd be on her way. All she had to do was lift her fist and give the door a good, solid bang.

Okay, so maybe she'd have to do a little more than that. Maybe after she'd knocked on Gray's hotel room door she'd need to offer a few flat-out lies along the line of, ''I haven't given you a thought in months'' and ''Gee, how time flies when you're out making merry with other men.'' Then she'd follow that with some incredible acting involving a couple of glances that said, ''You no longer interest me and you certainly don't rock my world anymore.'' And then she'd top it all off with a total purging of her normal personality. No emotional outbursts. No begging for one last kiss. And absolutely no shoving him onto the bed in order to have her wicked way with him. If she followed those few minor rules, she might make it through the next day or two.

She took a deep breath. She could do it. Sure she could.

She simply had to suppress any sort of reaction to Gray—particularly of the sexual sort—and present him with a cool facade. It would be a snap, even if she'd never managed it before. After all, she was a mature adult. She could act like it just this once, right? She lifted her fist to bang on the door, then dropped it again. Darn it. She didn't want to knock. She didn't want to be standing here at all, let alone preparing to deal with Gray and the fallout from their last meeting.

A door directly across from Gray's opened and an elderly woman stepped into the hallway. "Why, Emma Palmer," she exclaimed, blinking in surprise. "I was hoping to run into you. But I didn't expect it to be in the hotel corridor."

Emma turned around and pasted a bright smile on her face. "Hello, Widow Bryant. I didn't realize you were going to be in Seattle, too."

The elderly woman became known to everyone in Palmersville as Widow Bryant after losing her husband at the great age of twenty-five. Fifty years later her status hadn't changed, nor did it appear likely to anytime in the near future. In response to Emma's comment, she bobbed her head up and down in a birdlike motion. Everything about her seemed birdlike, from the flutter of her winglike hands to the feathery wisps of snowy hair floating around her rounded face.

"Tess invited me to her wedding, didn't she mention?" Widow Bryant asked.

A memory clicked. "Oh, that's right. You two started corresponding after her summer visits."

"We share a mutual interest in fund-raising. If it wasn't for Tess, I wouldn't have been able to get my literacy program off the ground."

"That sounds like her."

Widow Bryant leaned closer. "I wasn't going to attend the wedding," she admitted in a low voice. She glanced over her shoulder in a surreptitious manner and Emma fought to suppress a grin. Was she afraid Tess might somehow overhear? "You know how I hate leaving Bootsy behind."

Ever since Edgar Bryant had died, the widow and her succession of cats—always named Bootsy—had been inseparable. The latest cat had been a young, feisty tom when one of Palmersville's most talked-about scandals had occurred—the infamous skinny-dipping incident. Somehow the ornery tabby had given his owner the slip that day, the cat's timing proving fortuitous. With a single exception, everyone had walked away from the encounter thoroughly pleased.

Bootsy had experienced a rare moment of oat-sowing. Tess had won the skinny-dipping bet Emma had proposed without too many embarrassing repercussions. Raine had once again proven her amazing gift with animals by turning the cat on young Billy. And Billy Sheraton—the one exception—had received his just deserts in the form of four nasty claw marks across his hindquarters. But at least it had cured him of his Peeping Tom tendencies.

"I assume you decided to leave Bootsy behind after all and attend Tess's wedding?" Emma asked.

"To be honest, I read a description of the hotel and that convinced me to come. There was this lovely write-up of it last week in the newspaper. As soon as

I read it, I called Ellie and asked if she'd invite Bootsy for a visit. Ellie lives with Bootsy's momma, Buttercup.''

"That's right. I'd forgotten."

"No, you never have related to animals the way Raine does." She tutted sympathetically. "That's all right, dear. We love you, anyway."

A sudden thought occurred and Emma frowned. "I'm surprised you were able to find a room. This place has been booked solid for months."

"I was so fortunate. I got the very last room in the entire hotel. They said there was a last-minute cancellation." She tilted her head to one side. "Or was it a no-show?"

Emma gritted her teeth, comprehension dawning. "It was a no-show. *Someone* forgot to guarantee the room for late arrival with her credit card. Of course, if *someone's* flight had been on time and *someone's* luggage hadn't gotten lost, and *someone* hadn't taken three hours to fight through rush hour traffic to get to the hotel, she wouldn't have been a no-show."

Widow Bryant beamed. "And I wouldn't have gotten the room. Dear Edgar always said I had the devil's own luck."

Emma nodded morosely. "Yeah, me, too. But in my case, I don't think that's a good thing."

"So, is that your room?" Mrs. Bryant gestured toward the door across the hall. "How nice that we're neighbors."

Emma winced. Oh, dear. "Actually it's Gray's room," she admitted reluctantly. "Grandfather asked me to stop by and pass on a message before the wedding."

"Did he now." The widow flashed a knowing grin. "As excuses go, that one's as good as any, I suppose."

Great. Just great. No doubt it would be all over Palmersville that she'd been standing outside Gray's room shortly before Tess's wedding. From there it would be a small leap from outside Gray's room, to inside Gray's room, and an easy tumble from there to a claim that she was sharing Gray's bed. The gossip wouldn't spread in a mean or vindictive manner. No. Palmersville wasn't like that. It would just get exaggerated with each retelling.

"It's not what you think," Emma protested, determined to set the record straight.

"It never is, dear. Right up until you suddenly find yourself married with a half dozen young ones clinging to your skirts. Why I fought the inevitable tooth and nail. But my Edgar was impossible to resist."

Emma scowled. "I can resist Gray. No problem."

"That's the fighting spirit." Widow Bryant gave her the thumbs-up. "Keep telling yourself that if it'll make you feel any better. One word of advice and then I'll let you go. You only have a little over an hour before Tess's wedding, so don't get involved in too much hanky-panky or you'll be late. And then I won't be the only one putting two and two together."

No. No, no, *no!* "Please don't put two and two together!" Emma said in alarm. "And don't let anyone else put it together, either. That would be very bad. In this case two and two equals five."

"Only if you don't take precautions." The widow lowered her voice again. "There's a fully stocked shop in the lobby, just in case. Though knowing Gray, I'm certain he's planned for every contingency. Accountants tend to be like that."

Emma could feel her cheeks catch fire. "You still don't understand—"

"I wish I had time for you to explain it to me, but I have to run." Widow Bryant checked her hotel room door to make sure it had shut tight. "Interesting that you two are an item again. I would have thought it was over for good."

This got worse by the minute. "Again?" Emma asked weakly.

"Oh, I realize you tried to keep it quiet that last time. Not that it worked. You know how news gets around in a small town like Palmersville."

Emma released her breath in a rough exhalation. "Yes, I do know. That's because I'm the one who usually spreads it. But only the news I want to have spread is supposed to get spread." She turned to glare at Gray's hotel door. "Or so I thought."

"You can't expect people to keep quiet about your very first love affair. We were all quite excited for a while there. Until… Well, you know. After *that* we knew nothing would come of your relationship. Some were even taking bets on how it would all turn out."

"Bets!"

"I made a pretty penny, I'll tell you." She looked discomfited for a moment. "I hope you don't mind that I bet against you."

Wait a minute. *"Everyone* knew Gray and I were—" She choked on the words and tried again. "I mean, *thought* we had—"

"Not Tee, if that's what's worrying you," the widow hastened to reassure. "As far as I'm aware your grandfather never found out about your affair. Of course, no one had the nerve to tell him, either. We all knew he'd have had Gray's guts for garters. And as

tempting as that is after what Gray did, no one wants
to risk upsetting Tee. Not with his current health problems.''

Emma tried one last time. ''You don't understand.
There was nothing to tell. Nothing happened.''

''Of course not, dear. You stick to that story, too.
You never know. Someone might believe you.'' She
patted Emma's arm. ''Now, remember my advice and
keep your visit short and sweet or everyone will realize
the affair is on again and I won't get decent odds in
the next betting pool. I'll see you at the wedding.''
With a farewell flutter of her fingers, she headed down
the hall.

Emma cut loose with a decidedly unladylike exclamation.

Well, the damage had been done. There was no stopping the gossip now. She'd have to rely on Gray to
help stem what they could at the wedding. It wouldn't
take much. Unleashing their mutual dislike should do
the trick. Lifting her fist, she banged on his door. If
she pounded more vehemently than she might have
otherwise, blame it on frustration—a frustration she'd
be only too happy to take out on Gray.

The door swung open just as she was about to beat
on the door again. ''I thought I recognized that particular hammering,'' he offered in greeting. ''After all
these years I ought to.''

Time to choose. She could either sacrifice her pride
and throw herself into his arms, or she could take out
her irritation on him. It proved a tough decision, but
she managed it. Irritation won out. Aside from salvag-
ing her pride, getting angry would keep her from doing
something incredibly foolish—like finding the fastest
way to get him horizontal.

"This is all your fault!" she announced.

"Hello to you, too. Please." He stood to one side and waved an arm toward the sitting area of his hotel room. "Come in and make yourself comfortable while you yell at me some more."

"As tempted as I am to take you up on your offer, I don't dare." Not after what Widow Bryant had said. "If I stay any longer than five minutes everyone in Palmersville will think we're— We're—" A telltale blush blossomed across her cheekbones.

"Doing the dirty?" Gray offered, slamming the door shut behind her.

"That's disgusting!" Emma marched across the room, determined to put as much physical space between them as possible. That way she wouldn't be tempted to do the dirty, get down and dirty, play dirty, or do anything else that involved her, Gray, and stripping out of their clothes as quickly as possible. "But, yes. That's what I mean."

"Would you mind telling me why everyone in Palmersville would think we're doing the—"

"Indulging ourselves!" she inserted hastily.

"Fine. Indulging ourselves. Or am I supposed to guess?"

"If you hadn't arranged to have your hotel room directly across from Widow Bryant's, no one would suspect a thing."

"Hell. And here it took all my powers of persuasion to set that up." She heard his approach, could feel his presence a few short steps away. She shivered. He was close. Too close. "Just out of curiosity... *Why* did I set it up? Because I'm damned if I can remember."

Emma spun around to confront him, only to have every cogent thought tumble from her head. Heaven help her! Gray stood before her in a formfitting tux, his endless shoulders lovingly molded by the black silk. She remembered those shoulders. And why shouldn't she? She'd explored every inch of them. Kissed every inch. Slept on them. Wept on them. Clung to them during endless nights of passion.

She'd foolishly thought herself in love with him, mistaking lust for something deeper and more meaningful. What an idiot she'd been. Other than having been born in the same small town, they had nothing in common. Gray lived in a world that recognized two colors—black and white. Or perhaps, considering his accountant status, she should say black and red. Credit and debit. Plus and minus. He refused to see anything in between those two extremes, despite his name. It was an irony that hadn't escaped either of them. And while Gray busily organized his life into tidy little checkerboard boxes and compartments, Emma preferred something far different.

Her gaze returned to linger on his shoulders. At least, she preferred something other than what Gray had to offer right up until she'd walked into his hotel room. Perhaps one small relapse wouldn't be a total disaster. She could blame it on a stressful day, or an excess of emotion due to the marriage of one of her best friends. Or she could just admit that she was a sucker for broad shoulders, gorgeous blue eyes, lips capable of melting her into a puddle of feminine mush, and hands that could provoke the most outrageous reactions.

She moistened her lips. "Gray—"

She'd given herself away with that one aching word. His response hit hard, his eyes darkening with a mixture of painful yearning and ruthless determination. "If you don't stop looking at me I'm going to be disgusting

again,'' he warned. ''And if that happens, we're going
to miss Tess's wedding.''

Disgusting? Oh! *Doing the dirty.* Somehow it didn't
sound as bad as it had before. In fact, it sounded downright tantalizing. Not that she'd let Gray guess how she
felt. ''Hah! I knew it. Widow Bryant said we'd miss
the wedding if we weren't careful.''

He thrust a hand through his neatly combed hair,
rumpling the coffee-brown waves into uncharacteristic
disorder. It pleased Emma no end that she could provoke that sort of response from him. ''One of these
days we might have a conversation where I actually
understand what you're saying. Shall we try again?
Maybe we could approach this discussion logically.''

''Oh, right. Logic. Your specialty.'' Emma took a
deep breath, struggling to organize her thoughts into
some sort of reasonable order. Gray managed it as easily as blinking. But she'd never had much success with
something as bewildering as logic. ''Widow Bryant has
my hotel room and she's right across the hall from
you.''

Gray stared at her blankly. ''Your hotel room.''

''It was mine. But I arrived late and the hotel gave
it to her.''

He folded his arms across his chest. ''And how is
that my fault?''

''That part isn't.'' She scowled. ''And I guess the
fact that your room is directly across from hers isn't
your fault, either.''

''Grudging honesty. How refreshing.''

''Can the sarcasm, Gray. We have a problem.
Everyone in Palmersville thinks we had an affair.''

''We did have an affair.''

He was impossible. He'd always been impossible.

No doubt he'd keep it up until someone brought a short end to his impossible, miserable, accountant life. "Don't you understand?" To her distress, a hint of vulnerability underscored her words. "They're going to think we're still having one. Widow Bryant saw me come in here. The entire town is taking *bets* about the outcome of our relationship."

"Remind me to put some money down. Considering I know exactly how our relationship is going to come out, I can make a mint."

"Would you please be serious." She should laugh along. Any other time she would have. But she couldn't, not anymore. The misery of their parting prevented that. It hurt. Sometimes it hurt just to think. It even hurt to breathe. But to share the same space, to stand within inches of him and know she'd never again experience what they'd once had…. Ruthlessly she ignored the tide of painful emotions and forced herself to stick to the subject at hand. "Let me make this as black and red as I possibly can, so even you'll understand. I was seen outside your door."

"And?"

"And Widow Bryant assumes I'm here to visit you."

"You are."

"You know what I mean! She thinks we're doing the dir—" Emma groaned and covered her face in mortification. "Making love! She thought I came here to make love."

"So what if that's what she thinks?" His voice roughened. "And so what if that's what we actually do?"

He shouldn't tempt her like that. It wasn't fair.

"People would hear about it." She lifted her head and announced starkly, "*Tee* would find out."

He waved that aside, impatience implicit in the decisive gesture. "Let him. Hell, Emma. You're thirty years old. What difference does it make if your grandfather finds out about our affair?"

"Tee doesn't believe in affairs. He believes in marriage. If he finds out we've been—"

"Doing the dirty," Gray offered helpfully.

Anger ripped through her. "Darn it! Aren't you listening? He'll expect us to get married."

"So we'll refuse." He shrugged, unaffected by her annoyance, which irritated her all the more. "How hard is that?"

"You know Tee. He'll find a way. I'd rather not give him any excuse to beat a dead issue."

"That's going to be difficult if all of Palmersville is taking bets about whether or not we're—"

"We're not!"

"We were."

"Not any longer. And we're not going to start again, either."

"I'm real sorry to hear that."

The comment came so fast on the heels of her own that Emma knew he hadn't thought before speaking, or he'd never have admitted such a thing. She couldn't summon a single response, not in the face of such frankness. A flip, offhand comment would hurt him, while anything more serious would return to a place she didn't dare go.

For an endless moment their gazes locked in silent acknowledgment. They'd known each other almost all their lives. If she were honest, she'd admit that they knew each other better than any other two people.

They'd shared so many crucial occasions. Birthdays. Graduations. Anniversaries. Loss. Discoveries. The highest moments. The lowest. There wasn't a single important event in Emma's life in which Gray hadn't played a vital role, just as she'd been a major participant in all of his key milestones. The ghosts of countless memories stood between them, filling the air with the echoes of love and laughter and passion.

And regret.

"We don't have time for this, Emma. We have a wedding that starts in precisely one hour." His matter-of-fact comment succeeded in shattering the moment.

It was typical of him. Let a hint of emotion enter the relationship and he put a quick end to it. Although... She frowned. He didn't sound as though he was avoiding an emotional confrontation this time. If anything, he sounded exhausted. He'd been overdoing it lately, she'd bet her last dollar. Also typical. He always worked too hard, no matter how much she nagged at him about it. Well, it wasn't her problem anymore. She wouldn't give it another thought. She bit down on her lip. At least, she'd try not to.

"I'm well aware that the wedding starts in an hour," she finally acknowledged.

"Then what are you doing here, Emma?"

Slipping her purse off her shoulder, she fumbled through the paraphernalia that seemed to accumulate no matter how diligently she attempted to prevent it. Dislodging a slim envelope from beneath a calender book, a roll of breath fresheners, and headphones for her portable CD player, she offered it to Gray. "Here. This is for you. It's from Tee. He said it was urgent and that I should give it to you in private."

Gray accepted the envelope and ripped it open. It

only took a minute to scan the pertinent lines. *I got her there. What you choose to do with her is your business.* Great. Tee offered up his granddaughter, but he'd done it less than an hour before the wedding. The note must have been at the Cupid Committee's instigation. No doubt this was the "step one" Shadoe had referred to in his e-mail. Too bad the allotted hour didn't give Gray time to accomplish much of anything. At least, anything that would make a difference.

"What does he say?" Emma asked.

"It's business."

"Business." Her eyes narrowed in suspicion. "I used to work for Tee before I worked for you. If it's so urgent, I'm surprised no one's told me about it."

He considered for a moment. "It's also confidential."

"Confidential, as well as urgent. Interesting."

"Why the curiosity, Emma?"

She hesitated. "It's Tee. He—" She broke off, avoiding his gaze. "He hasn't been well recently and I'm worried. I just wanted to make sure the note didn't have anything to do with his health."

Gray studied her for an endless minute. She was keeping something from him. Something important. Time to find out what. "It doesn't have anything to do with Tee or his health," he reassured gravely. "But if it'll make you feel any better, I'll fill you in on what he said after the wedding. Will that satisfy you?"

She nodded. "Thanks. I'd appreciate that."

"No problem. Now tell me what's wrong with him."

"It's not that serious." Her lie was as transparent as ever. She'd never been able to put across a decent fib. He'd always regarded it as one of her more endearing qualities. "He'll be back to his old self in no time."

Gray closed the distance between them and dropped his hands to her shoulders. She didn't shrug off his hold, but a hint of defensiveness sparked in her eyes. They were strange eyes, tilted upward at the corners and cast in an exotic hue more gold than brown. They suited her, giving a catlike appearance to her triangular face. She was a wayward sprite, a golden changeling who had dropped into his life ages ago and irrevocably altered it. And it made him madder than hell.

He shouldn't be driven by such basic, physical urges. He wasn't the type. His was a simple world full of simple choices. Nor should he want to catch quicksilver or follow rainbows or chase futile dreams. Those were the desires of charlatans and con men. And yet, whenever he was around Emma that was precisely what he wanted to do. She stirred something primitive and ancient within him, breaching his defenses with a simple smile. Whenever she was around life seemed brighter, more full. He wanted the sort of life she promised.

He craved it.

He fisted his hands around the collar of her blouse and gathered the red-silk folds close beneath her chin. She'd compressed her mouth into a firm line, probably to keep it from trembling, though the rebellious expression in her eyes denied any such vulnerability. Wayward sprites tended to be odd creatures, both wary and bold. They were also as impossible to contain as sunshine or snowflakes. He'd learned that the hard way.

"What's wrong with Tee?" Gray repeated.

"We don't have time to discuss it now. We have to get to the church. You have no idea the day I've had. The airline lost my luggage and the hotel gave up my room. If Tess didn't have my bridesmaid dress, I'd—"

"What's wrong with Tee?"

He'd often found that the softer he spoke, the more dramatic the impact. Sure enough, the barely audible question had an instant effect. "He won't tell me." Her frustration was obvious. "I just know that he hasn't been feeling well and that he's seeing a doctor."

"Crosby?"

"Yes. Not that anyone tells *me* anything," she complained. "They don't seem to understand that patient confidentiality doesn't apply to granddaughters."

"I'll look into it."

She took instant exception. "I'm not asking you to look into it. I can take care of my own problems."

"I'll look into it."

"No." She jabbed his bow tie with her index finger. "For once in your life, you're going to stay out of my business. We don't have that sort of relationship anymore. We're not a couple. We're not involved. And we're certainly not doing the dirty, regardless of what all of Palmersville might think."

"But we want to."

"True—" Her eyes widened in sheer panic. "I mean, *no!* We don't. Not even a little."

"Too late." Releasing the collar of her blouse, he cupped her face. "Don't you know? You can't lie to me. You never have been able to. You still want me. Just as much as I want you."

And with that, he covered her mouth with his.

CHAPTER TWO

Subject: *WARNING! Hands off!*
To: *"Thomas T. Palmer"* <teepalmer@worldstar.com>
From: *Shadoe@CupidCommittee.com*
CC: *"Mr.Trouble"* <Grayson_Shaw@galaxies.net>
"Tess Lonigan" <tlonigan01@altruistics.net>
"Mayor Hornsby" <thebigcheese@worldstar.com>
BCC: *"Boss Lady"* <Adelaide@CupidCommittee.com>

A formal reminder to those of you who are trying to interfere in any matches currently under consideration by the Cupid Committee—manipulation of events will be regarded by the committee as a withdrawal of your request.

In regard to Emma Palmer: Matters are progressing, but we are reaching a critical juncture. It is imperative that no one intervene in events that have already been set in motion. We cannot be held responsible for any matchmaking failures, nor guarantee a positive outcome, if our requests are ignored.

Also, betting on the potential outcome is *strictly* prohibited. Odds are now running three to one against. Mayor Hornsby has asked that I remind you that only cash will be an acceptable form of payment for all bets. He also requests that Kevin McConnell pick up his goat at his earliest possible convenience.

Please forward to any other interested parties.

Shadoe, Cupid Committee Instigator, Fairly Extraordinaire

(Mother—am sending you this blind copy of the e-mail to Tee Palmer. It's critical that you speak to Tee or your plan will go down in flames. I'll deal with matters at my end. You were right. This is going to be a tough one. S.

P.S. Odds aren't bad. How much do you want me to put down?)

EMMA'S response to Gray's kiss was instantaneous.

A soft sigh slipped from her mouth to his. It was a sound she always made when he kissed her and he didn't realize how much he'd missed hearing it until that moment. Her head settled into the crook of his shoulder and he wrapped his arms around her in an uncompromising embrace. She didn't fight him as he half expected, but angled herself more tightly against him. They had always fit together well. That hadn't changed since their parting. If anything, their rapport added to the intensity, bringing a bittersweet urgency to the exchange.

Heaven help him, but she tasted good. He couldn't get enough of her particular flavor. It was downright addictive. He could get drunk on her, lose all thought and reason, not to mention every ounce of common sense. Not that he cared. As long as he had her back in his arms, nothing else mattered. He took his time renewing his acquaintance with her mouth. He especially loved her lower lip. It was wide and plump and soft, and he loved catching it between his teeth and tugging until she moaned. Sure enough a rumbling sound drifted up from deep in her chest, signaling her pleasure.

"This is a mistake. I need to stop you," she unsealed her mouth long enough to say.

The hell she would. "The hell you will."

She'd never taken opposition well. This proved no exception. "Don't worry. I'll get to it. Just give me another minute." She deepened the kiss, her lips parting and her tongue tangling with his. "Or maybe ten."

"Ten. Definitely ten."

Her heart thundered against his, the rhythm tattooing out a desperate demand. With every passing second, her body softened, relaxing into his, while her muscles tautened with desire. It formed a fascinating dichotomy, one he'd give anything to explore. But there wasn't time. Not that she showed any such reluctance. Her hands swept upward to trace the planes of his face. He turned his head slightly and dropped a kiss in the center of her palm.

He loved her hands. They were a reflection of her spirit, the fine-boned delicacy concealing an inner strength. Warmth invaded where she caressed, supplanting an inner cold he'd known since childhood. It was like spring overtaking the icy grip of winter. His reaction to her unique touch hit as strong and immediate as ever, stirring a primal need that he could neither stem nor deter.

Another sigh passed from her lips to his. "I've missed this." As always, her thoughts echoed his. He didn't know if it was because they had grown up together or if their brief time as lovers made them more closely in tune with each other. Right now, he knew what she wanted, could anticipate her desires almost before they formed in her head. "It's been so long since we were together."

"Too long," he agreed. "But we're done waiting."

"Good." Her hands shifted and he forgot to breathe. *Hell!* Where had she picked up that little maneuver? "No more waiting."

He held perfectly still beneath her grasp, fighting the urge to back her toward the bed and reacquaint himself with all he'd allowed to slip away. Damn, but he wanted her—wanted her naked and welcoming and as filled with the same sort of fierce, hot desire as he experienced every time he was around her.

The hell with it. They were both adults. Why shouldn't they enjoy the moment? He took a quick step toward the bed. Then another. Over Emma's shoulder he caught sight of an alarm clock. The digits were painfully large, blinking out a time that had him wincing. Forty-five minutes and counting. If he didn't stop now, they would miss the wedding and Emma would have one more reason to be annoyed with him. Annoyed? Missing her best friend's wedding would rate more than mere annoyance. Furious was closer to the truth. On the other hand, he'd have her in his bed again.

But for how long?

He swore beneath his breath. He didn't want her that way. He wanted all or nothing. Check that. He wanted it all. Which meant he had to control his randier impulses. It took every ounce of willpower to bring an end to their embrace. Pulling back, he gazed down into her face. She was gone. Totally gone.

He smiled as he tucked a strand of golden-brown hair behind her ear. "Still claiming you're not interested in doing the—"

"All right," she interrupted hastily. Her eyes flickered open, the color a rich, earthy brown gilded with brilliant sunshine. "Maybe I am interested in—"

"Just not now." He shrugged. "Okay by me. We'll have plenty of time after the wedding."

To his irritation, she shook her head. "Not a chance. We tried it once. It didn't work for us."

"Bull. It worked great."

"Okay, maybe that part of our relationship did." Her concession was the most reluctant he'd ever heard. "But that's the only thing that worked. Our personalities are too different. The way we approach life is as diametrically opposed as it's possible to get."

"That's the people of Palmersville talking."

"No, that's my conclusion after six months in your employ." She backed away from him. With each step that separated them she gained strength in her defiance. "It's not just what you did to Tee and the townspeople. Even if I forgave you for that, the underlying issue still stands between us."

"I didn't do anything to Tee or the townspeople," he thought to mention. Not that she listened.

"You pigeonhole us," she informed him. "As far as you're concerned, we fall into one of two categories. We're either roadblocks or opportunities."

Not this again. He might regard some people as roadblocks. He scowled at Emma. She was certainly giving an excellent imitation of one right now. But he didn't take advantage of people. Not ever. "This is old ground. We don't have time to go over it now."

"We never have time to go over it. If you don't agree with something I say, it doesn't get discussed."

"Works for me."

He shouldn't have been flip. Her chin lifted and her catlike eyes narrowed in obvious displeasure. "Well, it doesn't work for me. You can't pat me on the head like you used to when I was a child and dismiss my concerns.''

''I'm not dismissing—''

''Yes, Gray. You are.''

She folded her arms across her chest, stretching her blouse taut across her shoulders. Aw, hell. She was wearing red. Why hadn't he noticed before? He hated when she wore red. Red meant she was feeling defiant. Red meant something had gotten her back up.

Red always meant trouble.

Time for a strategic retreat. ''Emma, we have to get to the church.''

''In a minute. Do you remember my sixteenth birthday?''

Oh, man. This couldn't be good. ''How could I forget? I almost killed that kid. What was his name?''

''Eddie. Eddie McGwyre.''

''Little bastard. I should have taken him apart when I had the chance.''

''Do you remember why you tried to take him apart?''

''Hell, yeah.'' The image would be engraved on his brain for as long as he lived. ''He put his hands on you.''

''He kissed me. What you don't know, what you've *never* known is that he was supposed to kiss me. It was my sixteenth birthday and I'd planned it very carefully.''

It took a full minute to process her comment. ''You planned that…that mugging?''

''If you'd been willing to discuss what happened, if you hadn't patted me on the head and told me you knew what was best for me, you'd have figured that out long ago.''

Anger stirred. "You *planned* that mugging?" he repeated.

"I planned for Eddie McGwyre to give me my first kiss. Yes."

Of all the risky stunts. "Did you also plan for him to tackle you and practically rip your dress off?"

"Matters may have gotten a little out of hand," she conceded.

"A little?" There was no controlling his anger now. "If I hadn't rescued you, the events of that evening would have turned out far differently."

"No, they wouldn't have," she argued. "If you hadn't shown up I'd have kneed Eddie where it counts and he wouldn't have been in any shape to take events any further."

"Fine. You would have kneed McGwyre. You're—what?—five foot and a few laughable inches. Considering Mr. Football Star was six foot square and built like a tank, I'm sure your puny little knee would have done serious damage." Gray ripped at his bow tie. Somehow in the past few minutes it had managed to gain a stranglehold on his throat. "Would you mind explaining the point of this discussion?"

"You always think you know best."

"I knew best about McGwyre," he pointed out with amazing restraint.

"Yes, you did. But instead of letting me handle it, you took over. Instead of listening to my explanation, you dismissed my thoughts and opinions and concerns in favor of your own."

He stared at her blankly. "But mine were right."

"For you. Not for me."

Was she joking? She had to be. "Somehow I don't think the events of your sixteenth birthday are the best example. Not if you're trying to prove that you know best.''

"No, of course you wouldn't think that.''

She crossed to his side and busied herself repairing his bow tie. A hint of her distinctive perfume teased his nostrils. He remembered that scent. She used to dab it on right before they went to bed because she knew how much he liked it. His hands folded into fists and he carefully kept them at his side so he wouldn't drag her back into his arms. Did she have any idea the effect she had on him? She couldn't or she wouldn't dare come so close.

"Are you finished?'' he gritted out.

"Almost.''

"I suggest you hurry.'' Before he did something she'd regret. He wouldn't regret it. Hell, no. And she wouldn't until well after the fact. Of course, once she'd regained her senses, she'd take him apart brick by wrung-out, exhausted, satiated brick. And he'd let her, too, because by then he'd be too tired to give a damn.

"I've been thinking about our differences these past couple of months,'' she said in a conversational tone. "And after a while I came to realize that I'd never have made you a proper wife. I've always been a roadblock for you instead of offering the right sort of opportunities. I don't offer any pluses. I'd have been a negative in your little debit column and as soon as you realized that our marriage would have ended.''

"Not a chance.''

She patted his tie. "It's okay, Gray,'' she offered kindly. "What you did to Tee and the rest of the town was despicable, reprehensible, not to mention very bad. But I'm not upset about it anymore.''

"I'm glad to hear it.''

"We're better off apart." She crossed to the hotel room door and swung it open. "I'm sure you've figured that out by now, too."

"I'll tell you what I've figured out."

"I suggest you hurry or we'll be late." She tilted her head to one side. "Now that I think about it, you've never been late before, have you?"

"I've decided there's a first time for everything." Including taking care of a certain fire-engine red roadblock.

Reaching past her, he slammed the door closed again. He didn't bother arguing, debating, or discussing. He certainly didn't bother listening to any more of her explanations. Action always worked best for him. Sinking his hands deep into her hair, he tilted her head up to meet his. Then he kissed her again. She fell backward against the door, a delicious groan bursting from her throat. He followed her, imprinting himself on her in every conceivable way. By the time he was through he wanted her to remember every single moment she'd ever spent in his arms. Then let her try to claim they weren't meant to be together. It wouldn't take long to prove his point. He just had to be careful to stay in control of their embrace.

It took precisely two seconds to prove the fallacy of that plan. The moment their mouths collided they were both lost again. She breached his defenses with stunning ease, decimating protective devices that had held strong for years. With one kiss, one murmured word, one breathless laugh, he fell.

Hard.

The only saving grace was that she fell right alongside of him. "Don't tell me we're better off apart." The words sounded harsh and absolute, giving no quarter. Her earlier comments drifted through his head, taunting him. Black and red. Debit and credit. Plus and minus. No discussion or debate. Ruthlessly he shoved them aside. Didn't she understand? "How can we be better off apart when this is what happens every time we come together?"

"Gray—"

"No." He cut her off without compunction. "I've given you six months to see the error of your ways. I gave you too much time, by the looks of it."

She gazed up at him in total bewilderment. "What are you talking about?"

"Simple. Time's up, lady." Reaching behind her, he yanked open the door. "Run, hide, fight. I don't give a damn. I'm coming after you and nothing's going to stop me."

By the time Emma arrived at the church, she'd managed to calm down somewhat—at least enough to hide how flustered she was from Tess. Raine proved more discerning. As usual. She spared a quick glance in Tess's direction to make sure the bride wasn't paying attention before approaching and helping Emma change into her bridesmaid gown.

"What happened?" Raine demanded in an undertone. With swift efficiency, she zipped up the dress and gave the sash of the gown a small tug, settling it neatly at Emma's waist. "It's Gray, isn't it? What's he done now?"

"Nothing."

It wasn't a total lie. She was more ticked off at herself than Gray. All he'd done was kiss her. She'd been the one stupid enough to respond. Respond? *Be honest!* If he'd pointed her toward the bed, she'd have gone along without a single murmur of complaint. No doubt she'd have let him tumble her onto the mattress and have his wicked way with her. Afterward she'd probably have looked all pitiful and been stupid enough to quote Dickens. "Please, sir, I want some more." And it wouldn't be gruel she'd be begging for. When it came to Gray she was a total pushover.

"Earth to Emma." Raine snapped her fingers in front of Emma's face. "Are you sure Gray didn't do anything? You look...odd."

Uh-oh. "What do you mean?"

"You remind me of Bootsy after giving Widow Bryant the slip for a night of carousing."

Darn Gray! Emma fought the impulse to examine herself in the mirror. Knowing him, he'd left finger-prints somewhere. Or more likely she had one giant Grayson Shaw body print covering her from head to toe. After that kiss he'd planted on her, she wouldn't doubt it for a minute.

"You're imagining things," Emma muttered.

Amusement glittered in Raine's pale-green eyes. "Sure I am. That's why you have a whisker burn on your chin."

"Not a chance." She slapped a hand to her face. "He shaved before I got there."

Raine chuckled. "I gather having such intimate knowledge of Gray's grooming habits means you two are back together again."

"We most certainly are not," Emma maintained stoutly. "I learned my lesson six months ago."

Their relationship had ended in total disaster and neither of them wanted it resurrected. It was too painful. Her brows drew together. Of course, there was that small threat he'd made right before they'd left for the church. Something about her running or hiding or fighting. Something about coming after her. Something about not stopping. She shook her head. No doubt he regretted having said all that. He wasn't serious. He couldn't be. Gray had just been spouting off in the heat of the moment. And the moment had been hot. Steamy, sultry, passionately hot.

"Are you sure you learned your lesson?" Raine prompted. "You're looking a bit uncertain around the edges."

"That's only because of something Gray said. But he didn't mean it."

Raine nodded sagely. "Sounds just like him. He never means anything he says."

"Hah! A fat lot you know. Gray always means every word he—" Emma's eyes widened. "Oh, crud."

"Now that we have that cleared up, why don't we get you ready for the wedding?" Raine lifted Emma's hair off her nape. "Up or down?"

The change in subject came as a relief. Emma examined Raine's waist-length, straight black hair with a hint of envy. Her friend could be hit by a windstorm and when she emerged on the other side each strand would fall obediently into place. Emma, on the other hand, could brush hers into a perfect bell and within minutes look like she'd been the one in the windstorm.

"We better leave it down," she said. "There isn't time to get fancy."

Nodding in agreement, Raine picked up a selection of roses and baby's breath and carefully threaded them through Emma's hair. "So, did the airlines ever find your luggage?"

"No. Nor do I have a place to sleep tonight."

"You're kidding."

Emma shook her head. "The hotel gave away my room. I don't suppose you have an extra bed?"

"I'm not staying," Raine said apologetically. "I need to get home tonight, so I'm catching a red-eye."

Emma frowned in concern, relegating her own problems to the devil. Now that she thought about it, maybe she should consign Gray there, as well. "Is something wrong?"

"Hold still. Every time you move these flowers slide out." Raine anchored the roses in place with a handful of bobby pins. "To answer your question, nothing's wrong. We're shorthanded at the ranch and I don't want to leave my grandmother alone for any longer than necessary."

The door opened just then and the bridegroom's sister stuck her head in the door. "It's time," she announced. "Are you ready, Tess?"

Emma and Raine crossed to Tess's side and checked her over for any last-minute imperfections. Not that they found any. The bride looked stunning. She wore her red-gold hair in a sophisticated twist beneath a stylish little hat and veil. Her gown hugged her figure to just below her hips, then flared outward in a swirl of tulle and satin. It was striking and elegant and matched Tess's personality perfectly. She was also surprisingly calm.

"This is what I want," she explained with breathtaking simplicity. "Shayde and I fit together in all the right ways. I can't imagine spending the rest of my life with anyone else and I know that's how he feels, too."

Then there was no more time for conversation. Everyone gathered in the vestibule in preparation for the start of the ceremony. In a break with tradition, the groomsmen were escorting the bridesmaids up the aisle. Tess had claimed it gave the wedding a more "family" feel. It also left the poor groom, Shayde, standing at the altar with only the minister for company. Not that it seemed to bother him. He appeared as self-contained as ever.

"Since I missed the rehearsal, you'll have to fill me in," Emma whispered to Raine. "Who is everyone and how are we doing this?"

"You know Tess's brother, Seth. He'll be escorting Shayde's sister, Spirit. They'll go first." Raine indicated the young woman who had poked her head in the waiting room earlier. "Next you and Gray will walk up the aisle. And then I'll follow with Shayde's brother, Shadoe."

"Wait a minute. I know Shayde and Shadoe. But Spirit?"

Raine shrugged. "It's her middle name, though I haven't heard anyone actually call her that. Her mother calls her Harry. And her brothers call her sprite, pipsqueak, and 'hey you.'"

"Harry?"

Raine's mouth eased into a grin. "Didn't Tess tell you? Shayde's mother named her three children Tom, Dick, and Harry."

Emma's brows drew together. "But... Isn't their last name Smith?"

"You've got it."

"That's terrible!" Emma stared, appalled. "She named her children Tom, Dick, and Harry *Smith*? Doesn't she like them?"

"I gather Adelaide has a unique sense of humor. She claims she picked their names so she wouldn't have trouble remembering them." Raine allowed that to sink in before adding, "Their father chose their middle names."

"Shadoe, Shayde, and Spirit."

"Right. Tess said something about it being a throwback to Adelaide's hippy days. I gather she and her husband met when they were part of a commune or something."

"Good grief."

Raine shrugged. "It doesn't seem to bother any of them. And if you want my opinion, I think it suits their personalities."

There wasn't time for further discussion after that. Organ music swelled inside the chancel and the wedding coordinator shooed everyone into place. Emma assumed her position next to Gray. He took one look and a wide grin tugged at his mouth.

"What now?" she demanded in exasperation.

"Here." He twitched the flowers Raine had threaded through her hair into place. "That's better."

All right, so he could be a nice guy when he wanted. She'd give him that much. "Thanks."

"No problem. You look beautiful." He gave her a final once-over and a frown creased his brow. "Except—"

So much for being a nice guy. "Except *what?*"

"Your gown."

She glanced down at it. What had she forgotten? Shoes, hose, sash, neckline covering what it should be covering. No splotches, tears or wrinkles. Yet. As far as she could tell everything looked like it was in the proper place. "What's wrong with my gown?"

"It's red."

"So?"

He hesitated a moment before reluctantly conceding, "Whenever you wear red it always means trouble."

She grinned at that. Trouble. Good. Let him keep thinking that. Maybe it would give her a slight edge. When it came to dealing with Gray, she needed all the extra help she could get. "If you're worried, I suggest you don't do anything to tick me off."

"I wouldn't dream of it."

Apparently his idea of "not dreaming of it" didn't coincide with hers. The processional started toward the altar, Spirit and Seth in front. Emma paused beneath a flowered archway with Gray until the couple had reached the halfway point. Then she and Gray started their leisurely trip up the aisle.

"I've been thinking," he said in a conversational tone. "When we get married I'd like a big church wedding like this one."

CHAPTER THREE

Subject: It's not my fault!
To: Committee@CupidCommittee.com
From: Shadoe@CupidCommittee.com
CC: "Mr.Trouble" <Grayson_Shaw@galaxies.net>

You can *not* hang this one on me. Having Gray propose to Emma in the middle of Tess's wedding was *not—*I repeat*—not* my fault. I didn't instigate it. I didn't suggest it. Hell, I didn't even hint that he do anything so stupid. (Are you *trying* to screw this up, Gray?!?)

All consequences resulting from acts of sheer stupidity are to be laid firmly at the doorstep of the appropriate guilty party (Grayson Shaw, in case you haven't caught on).

In the case of dumb luck running smack-dab into unexpected success...I will accept credit for any positive outcomes resulting from the aforementioned act of stupidity.

Shadoe, Cupid Committee Instigator, Not-So-Extraordinaire

GRAY glanced at Emma to see how she took his comment. Hmm. Not well, if the bright-red splash of color sweeping across her cheekbones was any indication. "If we have a big wedding everyone in town can come," he offered in what he hoped was a conciliatory

tone of voice. Too bad he didn't do conciliatory very
well. Judging by Emma's expression, she didn't think
so, either. "They can even take bets on whether we'll
make it through the ceremony without a fight breaking
out."

She shot him a disgusted glance. "We're not going
to make it through *this* ceremony without a fight breaking out if you don't can the chitchat."

"This is August.... How does September or October
grab you? That way we can be settled in together before the holidays."

Something he'd said caused her to stumble. Or
maybe her heel had caught in the carpet runner. It
didn't look as if it had been tacked down very well.
He'd have to remember to mention it to the wedding
coordinator. People could be so sue-happy these days.
He tightened his hold on Emma to prevent any further
incidents.

In response her elbow managed to find its way into
his gut, jerking her free of his grasp. "I'm not marrying
you, Gray. And that's final."

"Final." He took a few measured steps to think that
over while he massaged his poor, abused ribs. "Final,
as in for now? Or final, as in for a few more months?"

Her fingers clenched around her bouquet. "Final, as
in forever. Final as it gets. Final as in I'm *not* going to
marry you. Not ever."

For some odd reason, she kept forgetting to use her
church voice. Not that Emma noticed. Gray shook his
head. But then, anger tended to do that to a person.
More often than not it caused a total breakdown in
appropriate behavior. Not that *he'd* point out
her error. Not a chance. Not while he was so busy
provoking that inappropriate behavior.

"So you're saying you probably won't marry me," he provoked a bit more. "Is that it?"

"Probably?" The breath hissed between her teeth. "Let me be perfectly clear. Not only won't I marry you, I wouldn't marry you if you were the last man on earth. I wouldn't marry you if we were the last two *people* on earth. Why, I wouldn't marry you if every shotgun on the planet were jammed against my back and I was given the option of marrying you or getting blasted to kingdom come."

He didn't bother asking who would be holding those shotguns if they were the last two people on the planet. Certain flaws in logic weren't worth analyzing. Besides, now that he'd gotten her so riled up, he might finally get some answers to the questions he'd been asking for the past six months—questions Emma had pointedly refused to answer. "And now you're going to tell me why you'd never marry me," he prompted.

"How can you even ask that?" The carpet runner reached up and snagged her heel again. This time, she allowed him to wrap his arm around her without threatening him with any more rib-breaking elbows. "You betrayed my confidence. I told you something in private and you used it to gain a business advantage."

"I see in hindsight that I probably should have discussed that with you first. But there was a time crunch involved."

"A time crunch?" She dragged him to a halt halfway up the aisle. "Meaning you only had a limited time to destroy my grandfather? Or was it that you only had a limited time to turn your infamous ruthlessness on the entire town? Or did you only have a limited time to make another billion dollars at the expense of those less fortunate individuals who got in your way?"

"Actually I lost a few million dollars because those less fortunate individuals who got in my way didn't know what the hell they were doing. They'd managed to run the business down to well below its fair market value. If I hadn't stepped in, your grandfather, not to mention half the town, would have gone bankrupt."

Emma slammed her flowers to the carpet. "That's a bald-faced lie! You take it back or I'll—"

"Do whatever the hell you want," he said coldly. "I don't lie. I don't cheat. And I don't con people."

"No, you just steal their businesses."

"And I don't steal."

"Then why do you own Tee's shoe factory instead of my grandfather owning it? And why is he so broken up about your taking away his business that he's practically at death's door?"

Finally. *"That's* why you're angry? Because of Tee? What did that old buzzard tell you? Because I'd be only too happy to set the record straight."

"Excuse me," Seth interrupted, returning down the aisle to join them. "In case you two hadn't noticed, we're supposed to be in the middle of a wedding ceremony. You do remember the wedding, don't you? Church, rings, an altar, a minister, a bride and groom waiting to get married. Does any of that sound familiar?"

"I *told* Gray I wouldn't marry him." Emma folded her arms across her chest. "And nothing you say will change my mind."

"Great. Except it's my *sister* who's supposed to be getting married."

Raine traversed the aisle, a silent Shadoe at her back. "They can't get married while you're blocking the aisle, Emma,'' she explained kindly. She waved for Spirit to join them. ''I'll tell you what. Why don't we get this settled real quick and then we can start the ceremony over.''

The four-year-old flower girl danced past, swinging her basket from side to side and deluging the guests with bright-red rose petals. The ring bearer—clearly her older brother—came charging after. Every few rows he stopped to scoop up flowers petals, attempting to shove them back into his sister's basket. Gray could have told him it was a losing proposition. The flower girl had ''mulish'' written all over her. He'd seen that expression often enough on Emma's face to be on close and intimate terms with it.

''There's nothing to settle,'' Emma announced. Her chin assumed an angle remarkably similar to the flower girl's. ''This is all Gray's fault.''

''As usual,'' he muttered.

''You're right. As usual. If you hadn't proposed—''

''Gray proposed?'' Widow Bryant piped up from a nearby pew. ''You realize that's going to change the odds, don't you? Could you do me a favor and keep the news quiet until I place a quick bet with the mayor?''

Tess approached from one end of the church, while Shayde approached from the other. ''Maybe we should conduct the ceremony from here,'' she suggested to the bridegroom.

His grim expression cleared, replaced by a slow smile. ''Honey, I'll take you anywhere I can get you. Front of the church, back of the church, middle of the church. You tell me where to go to say my 'I dos' and I'll be there.'' He looked at Gray, his smile fading. ''If you weren't one of my best friends I'd be busting your face about now.''

Gray nodded. ''And I'd deserve it, too.''

''Is there anything I can do to help move this along? I'd like to get married sometime soon.'' He checked his watch. ''Today, if possible.''

''You can tell Gray that I'm *not* going to marry him,'' Emma said. ''Maybe that will move things along.''

Shayde inclined his head. ''Gray, ol' buddy. I'm sorry to say, Emma is *not* going to marry you.'' He glanced at her. ''You do realize that Gray always gets what he wants no matter how many roadblocks crop up in his path? It's one of his defining qualities.''

''I'm well aware of that. Unfortunately for him, he's just hit a roadblock he can't budge.''

Gray rubbed his hands together. ''Good. A challenge.''

''Oh, dear,'' Tess murmured. ''It's never smart to out and out challenge them, Emma. I'd have thought you'd have learned that lesson by now.''

''I can tell you from personal experience it only makes them more determined,'' Raine added.

Widow Bryant waved her cell phone in the air. ''Mayor Hornsby says the odds are now two to one against a wedding between Gray and Emma,'' she called out. ''Any takers?''

''I like those odds,'' Emma retorted. ''Put me down for fifty.''

Gray shook his head. ''You're throwing your money away on that one. It's a bad bet.''

''There's nothing you can do or say that will convince me to marry you. Therefore, it's an excellent bet.''

"We'll see." He turned to the rest of the wedding party. "Anyone else care to place a bet?"

There was some general shuffling of feet and a few hesitant glances toward Widow Bryant. "Put me down for twenty in Gray's favor," Shayde said.

"Ten dollars says Gray has her married before the month's out."

Emma swung around to confront Tess. "How could you!"

"Sorry, sweetie. Having been in your spot not so long ago, I've learned my lesson. You don't have a hope of winning this one."

One look at Emma's face warned Gray that they had pushed matters as far as they could be pushed. Bending down, he picked up her bouquet and handed it to her. The flowers were a bit the worse for wear after their abrupt collision with the floor, but they would do in a pinch. And this was definitely a pinch.

"Oh, no." She stared at the bouquet in alarm. "Look what I've done."

Gray didn't like the sound of this. Knowing Emma, she wasn't just upset about the flowers. It was beginning to dawn on her that she'd disrupted her best friend's wedding. He didn't doubt that guilt would rapidly set in and if that happened, tears wouldn't be far behind. If he didn't want the ceremony to turn into a complete disaster, he needed to act. Fast.

"They're not so bad," he reassured. He straightened a dejected white rose, and awkwardly patted a sprig of baby's breath into place. He also managed to further mangle the white-satin bow, but with luck, Emma wouldn't notice. "There. Almost as good as new." He offered a bracing smile. "Now what do you say we get this show on the road?"

His suggestion met with instant approval. Mass confusion reigned for the few minutes it took everyone to reassemble, which succeeded in distracting Emma. This time when they made the trip up the aisle, Gray didn't say a word, not even when she shot him several pointed sidelong glances. But as they took their stances on either side of Tess and Shayde, and listened while the timeless vows were spoken, Gray kept his gaze fixed on his bride-to-be.

Soon. Soon he'd have this nonsense with her grandfather straightened out and then he and Emma would be speaking those exact same words. The Cupid Committee had never failed yet. They weren't going to start with his wedding. No matter what the odds, no matter what it took, Emma would be his.

Gray caught hold of Emma's elbow. "This has to be the worst reception I've ever attended." He towed her out of House Milano's huge dining area, past the dance floor, and through a gated archway that divided the two sections of the restaurant. He paused beside a bank of windows that stretched floor to ceiling. From their location perched high atop King Towers, they commanded an unparalleled view of Seattle and Puget Sound. Not that Gray seemed to notice. "And now that I consider the matter, the wedding wasn't all that great, either."

Emma winced. He didn't sound happy. In fact, he sounded downright furious. She just wished he'd take his anger out on her in the middle of the brightly lit, heavily peopled section of the restaurant, instead of here. In the distance she could still hear the music and chatter emanating from the reception. But in this private, more dimly lit area the sounds had grown muted, intensifying the impression of being trapped in their own little world.

"I assume you're blaming me for what happened at both the wedding and reception?" Emma demanded.

"I can't think of anyone else to blame."

"I can. Let's start with *you*." She jabbed the onyx stud decorating his snowy-white dress shirt. Over his shoulder the lights of the city glittered like fallen stars, extending even into Puget Sound where the ferries were glowing embers drifting across an ink-black expanse of water. "If you hadn't made that crack at the wedding ceremony about getting married—"

His jaw poked out an inch. "It was an innocent remark made in passing. Casual conversation while we walked up the aisle."

She couldn't believe Gray had the nerve to say that. "It was neither innocent nor was it casual. You declared your intentions loud and clear in front of half the world." He lifted an eyebrow at the exaggeration and she released her breath in an irritated rush. "Okay, half of Seattle. That doesn't change the fact that you had no business starting something in the middle of Tess's wedding."

"I wasn't the one who came to a dead halt partway up the aisle and threw her flowers to the floor."

"I'm not going into that with you again. I apologized to Tess. Fortunately she has a wonderful sense of humor." Too wonderful. She'd taken Gray's foolishness as a serious marriage proposal.

"And lucky for you Shayde has a wonderful sense of humor, too. After sharing many of my misspent college days with him, I can guarantee that you wouldn't want to get on his bad side."

This was ridiculous. "I have better things to do than

stand around and argue with you. This conversation is at an end.'' Swinging away, she marched deeper into the darkened expanse of the restaurant. To her annoyance, Gray fell into step beside her. ''You can't come with me,'' she warned.

''Sure I can.''

''Not where I'm going.''

Someplace around here was the closet containing the street clothes she'd worn when she'd flown in this morning. Too bad she had such a lousy sense of direction. Before she was forced to remind Gray of her impairment, an elderly gentleman appeared in front of her. Dressed formally in a tux, he had a perfect white rose pinned to his lapel.

''Good evening, Ms. Palmer. Mr. Shaw. Welcome to House Milano.'' He offered them a courtly little bow. ''How may I be of service?''

Emma blinked in surprise. ''You know our names?''

''You'll find that Giorgio knows everyone's names,'' Gray explained. ''He's renowned for it.''

A small smile played about the older man's mouth. ''You flatter me, Mr. Shaw.''

''He's also renowned for protecting the reputation of House Milano. In fact, last time I was here Giorgio was almost forced to throw me out.'' He leaned closer to Emma. ''Shayde and I weren't behaving very well.''

''We don't allow schoolboy scuffles in the restaurant,'' Giorgio confirmed.

He'd snagged Emma's interest with that little tidbit. ''Gray and Shayde were in a fight?''

''Shayde started it,'' Gray explained. ''I merely defended myself.''

''What was your argument about?''

He shrugged. ''My good old buddy seemed to think

Tess and I were involved. He didn't understand that I'm a one woman kind of man."

Not that again. Time for a strategic retreat. She addressed Giorgio. "I seem to have lost my things. I know I stuck them in a closet someplace around here. Have you any idea where?"

"Right this way, Ms. Palmer."

Opening a nearby door, he removed a bag containing the clothes she'd donned earlier that morning, along with her purse. "There's a ladies' room around the corner," he said, handing over her possessions.

"Thank you," she murmured.

"If there's anything else you need, don't hesitate to ask." With that, he disappeared as silently as he'd arrived.

Emma's hands curled around the paper bag. Was it only this morning that she'd left Palmersville? She'd been filled with such excitement, and yet nothing had turned out the way she'd hoped. Instead of spending a special day with her best friends, she'd spent those hours trapped in an airport, on an airplane, and in a cab. Unexpected tears pricked her eyes. Today was supposed to have been a final bonding between three women who were more like sisters than friends. And she'd missed out on that. Worse, she'd done her level best to turn Tess's wedding into a total disaster.

She shot Gray a condemning glance through her tears. She'd done her level best to turn it into a total disaster with a little help. "If you'll excuse me. I have to change."

"You're not crying, are you?" he questioned in concern. "Aw, hell. Listen to me, Emma—"

Not giving him time to start a new discussion—not that Gray ever did much discussing, his specialty came in the form of sweeping commands—she rounded the corner and shoved open the door to the spacious ladies' room. Once again he proved her right. He didn't bother discussing anything. He simply followed behind.

She turned on him in disbelief. "You can't come in here."

"Why not?" He cupped her chin and tilted her face to the light. Gently he swept his thumbs beneath her eyes, gathering up the evidence of her tears. "What's wrong? Why are you crying?"

Emma fought the urge to tumble into his arms as she had when she was younger. When would she learn? She didn't belong there anymore. The thought threatened more tears and she forced herself to step away from Gray. Maybe if she kept her distance she'd have better success controlling her emotions. Better yet, if she could get him to keep his distance it would solve all her problems. "I don't want to discuss it," she said. "Please go away."

"I'm not leaving you in tears."

"I'm not in tears anymore. And you have to leave. In case you haven't noticed, this is the women's room. Men aren't allowed. And last time I checked you still qualified as male. Though I'd be happy to try to correct that if you'd like." Her gaze dropped suggestively. "Do you think the maneuver I was going to use on Eddie McGwyre would work on you?"

"Not a chance."

"In that case, you have to leave."

"Why?"

Why? "Because," she sputtered. "You're not allowed to be in here. You'll get in trouble." Good one, Emma. That was sure to convince him to leave.

He looked around. "I don't hear any alarms. And no one's fainting in shock."

"That's because there's no one in here to faint."

"Except you."

Fortunately their verbal sparring had eased the threat of tears, enabling her to face him with most of her usual temerity intact. "I'm not the fainting type."

"Then there's no problem."

He took a seat in the small lounging area. Sprawled in the overstuffed chair in such an intensely feminine place accentuated his masculinity. He looked big and dangerous. Without question, he posed a serious threat to her well-being. He wanted something and she had a sneaking suspicion it involved her. More than a sneaking suspicion considering his marriage proposal.

She tossed her purse onto the counter beside him and yanked her clothing from the bag. "Come on, Gray. Get lost. I have to change."

"I'm not stopping you."

"Darn it! How many times do I have to tell you? You're not supposed to be here."

"We haven't finished our discussion." He yanked at his bow tie, unraveling it with a single tug. A half dozen onyx studs came next, his shirt gaping in a most intriguing fashion. He dropped the studs beside her purse on the counter. "And why are you changing? You look fine in your bridesmaid dress."

She dragged her gaze from the expanse of chest he'd exposed. No doubt it was a deliberate attempt on his part to rattle her. So what if it was working? And so what if he knew it? She could still hold her own in a discussion with Gray. She just needed to make sure she stayed out of touching range. "You mean, I look fine despite the fact that my dress is red."

"Right. Despite that."

"I'm changing because I'm going home."

"Home."

He didn't like her answer. He stirred in the chair, reminding her of nothing more than a large, irritated predator. How did he do that, anyway? Without saying a word he managed to communicate his displeasure in a manner that would have the average mortal running for cover. But not her. She locked her knees in place. No, way. Fortunately she'd known him long enough that his patented frowns no longer bothered her. Nor did the blatant tensing of all his impressive muscles or the hard look darkening his gorgeous blue eyes.

At least, they didn't bother her much.

"Why are you going home?" he asked.

"Raine is flying back to Texas tonight. She offered to share a cab to the airport with me and I thought it would give us time to spend together since we didn't get the opportunity before the wedding. I also don't have a hotel room for tonight. So it seemed logical to go home." She offered her sweetest smile. "Logic. You should appreciate that."

"You can always spend the night with me."

"Right. With Widow Bryant across the hall ready to report to all of Palmersville that we were doing the—" Darn Gray! He'd stuck that phrase in her head and now she couldn't get it out. "Thanks, but I don't think so."

"Just a thought."

She disappeared into one of the cubicles and struggled with the zip closing her gown. "Why are you really here? What's so urgent that it couldn't wait?"

"The list is long and detailed."

Emma grinned as her zip gave way. "Now why doesn't that surprise me?"

"Because you know me far too well."

She couldn't argue with that. He'd always been organized. Perhaps that's why he was so successful at being ruthless. He probably had it down to a formula or a mathematical equation or something. Number one: state your demands. Number two: state your demands in a softer voice in order to scare the hell out of everyone. Number three: when demands aren't met, find a way over, under or around any and all obstacles.

"Are you still there?" Gray asked.

Had his voice grown softer? Nah. Must be her imagination. "Go ahead and tell me what's topping that list of yours. We wouldn't want to skip over anything important or cross stuff off in the wrong order."

To her surprise, he didn't respond to her teasing. "First, I'm sorry about what happened at the wedding. I didn't mean to start a commotion."

Emma yanked the door open a crack to see if he was serious. He was. Dead serious. "Apology accepted. What about the reception?"

He shook his head, his expression turning stubborn. "That wasn't my fault."

She let him know her opinion about that by banging the door to the cubicle closed again. "You're probably the only person at the reception operating under that misconception. You took a simple tossing of the bride's bouquet and turned it into a free-for-all."

"I wasn't the one who demanded a retoss."

She stepped out of her gown and slung it over the door of the stall. "I only did that because there was interference on the playing field." Shoving her arms into the sleeves of her blouse, she worked the buttons. For some reason, the row of tiny pearls refused to slide into the appropriate holes. No doubt it was Gray's fault.

She'd be at a loss to explain why, but that didn't change her conviction any. "Tossing the bouquet is not a volleyball game. You had no right to use your special skills to affect the outcome. And don't bother asking what special skills. You know perfectly well you're an expert when it comes to volleyball."

"It was an innocent tap."

"Innocent, my aunt Fanny. That was play 7B with a twist." Kicking her shoes under the door, she yanked on her slacks. "I'd recognize it anywhere."

"The bouquet would have hit the floor if I hadn't batted it into the air again. I was just being a considerate guest."

"Uh-huh." She thrust the tails of her blouse into the waistband of her slacks. "That's why you shouted, 'Use your elbows, Emma! There's no referee!' You were being a considerate guest."

"Hey, you didn't have to jump. But I noticed you leaped like a gazelle, even in those heels."

"Instinct!" She banged open the stall door and escaped the cubicle. "You've heard of instinct before, haven't you? How many years have we practiced that play?"

He grinned smugly. "It never fails, does it?"

She picked up one of her shoes and shook it at him. "Tell that to the poor woman with the orange-and-purple hair. You almost knocked her down when you intercepted the bouquet."

"Not a problem. She wasn't going to get married next, even if she'd caught it. No point in giving her false hope."

"That's terrible!" She hopped up and down on one foot as she struggled into her shoe. Darn it, where had the other one disappeared to? She couldn't have kicked it that far. "You're not usually so cruel, Gray. What's gotten into you?"

"I'm being honest. There's not a chance in hell that woman will ever marry. I'm not even sure she wants to. Not only wasn't she one of the wedding guests, but I think she was in there as a spoiler."

"Oh, please!" Emma finally spotted her other shoe lying drunkenly beneath one of the sinks. "How can you possibly know that?"

He ticked off on his fingers in typical Gray-at-his-most-logical fashion. "First, she wasn't at the wedding. I'd have noticed if she had been. That hair of hers is hard to miss. That means she was crashing the reception. It happens sometimes."

"Maybe she was running late and missed the ceremony."

"Nope. I overheard Tess's mother asking. No one knew her."

Emma shoved her foot into her remaining shoe and bent to fasten the straps. "You still haven't explained why she wouldn't ever marry."

"I was getting to that." He ticked off on another finger. "And second, she had letters tattooed across her knuckles. Big hairy knuckles, I might add."

"So?"

"The letters spelled out man hater. At least, I think it was man hater. All that hair made it hard to read." He tilted his head to one side. "I suppose it could have been man eater. In either case, there was an exclamation point after the 'r' and a skull and crossbones on her pinky. No way was she getting Tess's bouquet. Not while I was around to prevent it."

"It was still interference and still deserved a retoss."

"Says you."

"Right. Says me." Emma gave up arguing and glanced at her purse.

She was changed and ready to leave. All that remained was to collect her bridesmaid dress and grab her purse from off the counter next to Gray. He might still want to do a bit more discussing, but she planned to take the coward's way out and bolt at the first opportunity. There was only one problem with that plan, and he sat blocking the exit.

As though aware of her intentions, Gray climbed to his feet and approached. An unexpected tightness gripped her throat. When had he grown so big and intimidating? He'd always been uncomfortably tall, but she'd figured her own lack of inches was responsible for that impression. And despite everyone in Palmersville having found him unnerving from the time he'd escaped adolescence, she never had.

Until now.

"Time for the second item on my list," he informed her.

Was that a warning? "And what's that?" She tried for a show of bravado and failed miserably. If she'd been a dog, her tail would have been tickling her tummy right about now.

"You. You're second on my list."

CHAPTER FOUR

Subject: What were you thinking?
To: "Screy-up Extraordinaire"
Shadoe@CupidCommittee.com
From: Grayson_Shaw@galaxies.net

You said you'd take care of things. You didn't say you'd make her cry! Do you have any idea how much she was looking forward to spending time with Raine and Tess? You couldn't come up with a better plan than to make her miss her flight? And you also made her lose her hotel room. Where's she supposed to spend the night? With me? How are you going to pull that one off? I'm not impressed, Shadoe.

Gray

Subject: Re: What were you thinking?
To: "Mr.Trouble" Grayson_Shaw@galaxies.net
From: Shadoe@CupidCommittee.com

This is the problem when amateurs get involved in the matchmaking business. I warned you that it wouldn't work if you knew too much. But would you listen? No!

And let me tell you one more thing... Considering what you pulled at the wedding and reception, you have a hell of a nerve complaining about my actions. So listen up, old buddy. On the off chance you've overlooked the obvious, *I'm* the Cupid Committee Instigator. That means *I* instigate the matches. Not *you*. Now stay out of my business or you can kiss this match goodbye!

Shadoe, Cupid Committee Instigator

EMMA fell back a pace. "I'm afraid you'll just have to cross me off your list." Her voice sounded odd, as though someone had muted the volume. How annoying. She cleared her throat and tried again. "I'm supposed to meet Raine by the elevators as soon as I've changed. In case you haven't noticed, I'm now wearing a different outfit than when I first came in here. That means it's time for me to leave."

Gray parked himself in front of her in all of his big, intimidating glory. "Raine will have to wait."

"I'm not sure she can. She has a flight in just a few—"

"You were crying earlier," he interrupted. "Why?"

Emma shook her head. "I told you I didn't want to discuss it."

"Maybe I can guess."

Why didn't he let her go? Why did he have to keep pushing when all she wanted was to be left alone. "I wish you wouldn't."

"I've known you for a lot of years, remember? There used to be a time when we didn't keep secrets from each other. A time we could tell each other anything." He spoke in a low tone, holding her in place with a painful mixture of frustration and urgency. "Now I'm reduced to guessing what's wrong."

"That's because our relationship has changed. You changed it. Or have you forgotten that minor detail?"

"And you don't handle change well, do you? That's why you're upset. It's because everything's different now. Tee and Palmer Shoes. The two of us. Your relationship with your friends. Nothing's the same anymore."

She didn't bother to deny it. Why should she? It was the truth. "I'll adjust. I always do."

"How? By cutting yourself off? By cutting off the people who cause you pain?" He came a step closer. "Listen to me, Emma. Tess isn't leaving you."

"I know."

"I'm not sure you do." He dropped his hands to her shoulders. "Hear what I'm saying, sweetheart. She's not leaving you."

"She's just getting married," Emma retorted impatiently, wriggling beneath his hold. "Yes, I know."

He didn't release her. Instead his thumbs moved in a hypnotic circle, massaging the tense muscles across her collarbone. "Your head knows, but I don't think your heart is paying attention. Tess isn't leaving you. This isn't like when your parents died."

"Of course it's not. Tess isn't dead—" To Emma's horror, her voice broke. It took a critical few moments to recover and once she had, the truth escaped of its own volition. "But it feels like it."

He pulled her against his chest and simply held her. "You lost your parents when you were only five. Even though Tee and Lizzie took you in and gave you a secure home, it didn't last. Your grandmother died when you were twelve. That's a lot of loss to deal with at such a young age. It's no wonder you don't like change. No wonder you run from it."

"I don't run."

"You may not consider it running. When you were little and something happened to upset your world, you'd go hide in the tree fort Tee and I built by Nugget Creek. You might not still go there physically, but you do emotionally. You escape to someplace familiar and safe, and hide there until the pain goes away."

"It's called a rut and ruts are good," she explained. The words were muffled against his open dress shirt, but he seemed to catch them. "Ruts are comfortable."

A tender laugh rumbled through his chest. "Not when you're the only one in that rut." He tilted her face upward. "I'm still here, sweetheart. You still have your grandfather, despite his current bout of ill health. And you still have your friends. None of us are going anywhere. I promise."

"But it won't be the same. Not ever again." Didn't he understand? "I missed those last few hours with Tess and Raine. And I can't get them back."

"I'm sorry, Emma. I wish there were something I could do to fix it."

She shook her head, determined not to give into weakness—a six-foot-one, blue-eyed, brown-haired weakness of the worst sort. "You can't. It's not in your job description, anymore."

"It could be."

"What we had is ov—" He slid his hand along the curve of her cheek and coherent thought slipped away. Her eyes drifted closed as she struggled to bring her brain back on line. What had she been about to tell him? Oh, right. "What we had is—"

His fingers drifted past her temple and forked deep into her hair, dislodging the flowers pinned there. His touch succeeded where all else had failed. It only took that single gentle caress to quiet the jumble of words forming in her mind. She fell silent, all rational thought transposed into sheer emotion. Desire stirred deep within, awakening a need that only one man could sate. It spread outward, sweeping through every vein and pore. His essence filled her, overwhelmed her, conquering any and all resistance. More flowers fluttered to the floor, the red-and-white petals forming a circle that closed them off from the rest of the world. Bound them as though in some ancient rite.

"You can run away, but that won't change anything," he murmured.

"I'm not running," she whispered. How could she? She was trapped within a ring of flowers, his arms forming an unbreakable bond. She couldn't escape, not without violating the ring of flowers that held them.

"Sure you are. You're running for all your worth. But I'm coming after you and I won't give up. I won't leave you, Emma. Not ever."

He knew her too well. Knew which buttons to push to gain a reaction. Was nothing sacrosanct with him? Was he so ruthless that he'd do anything to get his own way? "Why are you doing this?"

"Because I want you."

"Want isn't enough. We found that out six months ago."

"It's a start. If we treat it carefully, it can become something more."

"Let me go, Gray."

"I wish I could." His head lowered to hers. "But I can't."

His kiss was a promise, a promise as absolute as the words Tess and Shayde had exchanged at the altar. It spoke of hope and faith and a forever kind of love. It made a commitment she couldn't allow because she didn't trust his motivation, couldn't trust that he wouldn't betray her again.

"No." She tore free of his arms and escaped the enchanted circle of flowers. "For whatever reason, you've decided you want me for your wife. But it doesn't matter what I want, does it? Once you've made up your mind, that's the end of it. I either fall in line or you'll find a way to make me."

He didn't say a word. He didn't have to. Tension rippled across the expanse of his shoulders and closed his hands into fists. Somehow, probably through sheer dumb luck, she'd hit on the truth.

"I'd never use force," he finally said.

"But you'd find a way to accomplish your goal, wouldn't you?" Emma crossed to the cubicle where she'd changed and snatched her bridesmaid dress from off the door. Not quite sure what else to do with it, she stuffed it into her oversize purse. It didn't fit very well. The brilliant-red silk spilled over the top and trailed toward the floor. "I'm leaving. And I don't want you following me. What we had is over. Deal with it."

"You love me, Emma. You have since you were a teenager."

Her mouth tilted to one side in a half smile. "What's that got to with anything. I love chocolate, too."

"Meaning?"

"As much as I love chocolate, I can't eat it. It doesn't agree with me except in small doses."

"I'm not chocolate."

Her smile grew. "You're not just chocolate, Gray. You're deep, dark double rich fudge. I can't even look at you without knowing that one bite will cause me more trouble than it's worth.''

Without another word, she turned and left the women's room, red silk and flower petals trailing in her wake.

Gray stood for a long moment watching a final few petals drift to the floor. "I've got news for you, honey. Trouble or not, you're going to learn to like fudge. Hell, one way or another, you're going to learn to love it.''

Shadoe flipped open his cell phone and punched in a number. "Yeah, it's me.''

"Is everything set?'' Adelaide asked.

"I've done just what you asked. But I don't like it. What if something goes wrong? Emma could get hurt.''

"Nothing is going to go wrong and no one will get hurt.''

"Maybe I should stick with her until—''

"I told you this would be a tricky match.''

He grimaced. "So you did. But I'm not used to taking a back seat.''

"You Instigators are all alike. You seem to think no one in the world can manage a simple love affair without your help.''

"Why do you think the divorce rate is so high? Because there aren't enough good Instigators arranging appropriate matches.''

"And what about a match for you?''

His dark brows drew together. "What do you mean?''

"I just wondered when you were going to get around to instigating a match for yourself. I wouldn't have to spend my life interfering in everyone else's business if I had grandchildren to keep me busy."

Hell. There were times when working for his mother could be a serious drawback. This was clearly one of them. "First, I'm not interested in finding someone for myself. I made that perfectly clear when I joined the business. You do remember that was one of the conditions of my employment, don't you?"

"I vaguely recall something about that," Adelaide admitted.

"Damn right. Second, you have Tess and Shayde to provide you with all the grandchildren you need. And if they don't take care of it, you can go bother Spirit. You'll either have your head handed to you, or you might get lucky and she'll start popping babies."

"I prefer she get married before she starts popping anything. And third?"

"What makes you think there's a third?"

"I know you, Shadoe. You're just like Gray. There's always a third."

"Third. You could have a hundred grandchildren and you'd still be a modern day Cupid. You can't resist."

"That's because I'm a romantic at heart." She paused a beat. "Just like you, dear."

Before he had a chance to explain how completely wrong she was, she hung up. "I'm not a romantic," he shouted in frustration. "I just like messing around in other people's business."

He glared at his cell phone. Typical. He finally knew exactly what he wanted to say to her and she hung up. And no doubt she was laughing her fool head off at his expense, too.

Mothers. He flipped his phone closed. Can't live with 'em. Can't join the planet without 'em.

Yet.

Emma slammed the door of the cab closed and turned to face the King's Crown hotel. Bright, friendly lights shone through the pouring rain, but she couldn't decide if they were in welcome or designed to taunt her. With a roar, the cab pulled away from the curb, its rear tires spinning on the slick pavement and sending a spray of water into the air. It came down directly on Emma. Not that it mattered, she decided grimly. It wasn't like she could get any wetter. Or dirtier.

The automatic doors of the hotel swept open and she limped into the foyer. Of course, with one heel snapped off and the other missing a strap, limping was the only way she could maneuver. She tromped across the spot-less marble entrance toward the elevators, not daring to look left or right. She also didn't dare glance behind her. She could guess what she'd find—a sluglike trail of slime and dirt.

"Excuse me, Miss." An alarmed voice came from the direction of the reservation desk. "Could you check in, please? Miss?"

Emma ignored him, which probably wasn't the smartest choice. An instant later she heard the recep-tionist requesting security. She picked up her pace. She'd kept her fingers crossed that no one would try to stop her, though she could now kiss off that partic-ular fantasy. She wasn't a guest. She didn't have a purse or any sort of identification. And aside from be-ing soaked from head to toe, the front of her once red, now black, slacks and blouse had done an excellent job of polishing the floor of the airport. Who knew those floors could get so dirty? To the receptionist, she probably looked like some crazed street person intent on invading their exclusive hotel.

Making her way to the bank of elevators, she lurched into a car just as someone from security came hustling into the lobby. She stabbed the button for the thirty-third floor and then jammed her thumb on the "close door" button. For the first time that day something went right. The elevator door swept shut and the car began a meteoric rise toward the hotel's upper floors. A dirty puddle of water pooled at her feet as the floor numbers ticked off and Emma stepped clear of the puddle only to have another one form beneath her new location. Damn. At this rate, they would be able to track her without needing so much as a bloodhound. Just follow whatever disgusting bits and pieces dripped off her.

The elevator lurched to a stop and Emma escaped the car, hurrying along the corridor as fast as her broken heel and snapped shoe strap would allow. She hesitated outside of Widow Bryant's door. It was late and no doubt the elderly woman had gone to sleep long ago. But old people didn't sleep soundly, did they? Tee had complained often enough about age-related insomnia. Sparing a quick glance over her shoulder at the door directly opposite the widow's, Emma rapped as softly as possible. With luck Gray wouldn't hear.

"Widow Bryant? Are you there? It's Emma." The seconds ticked by without a response and she knocked a little harder. "It's Emma Palmer. I need help."

At the far end of the corridor the elevator pinged, warning of someone's arrival. What if it was security? Taking a deep breath, she gave up on caution. If security planned to toss her out of the hotel, she might as well give them just cause. Balling up her hand, she banged for all she was worth.

"Widow Bryant?" she shouted. "Please open the door."

Across the corridor the door crashed open, and with a sigh of resignation, Emma turned to face Gray. One look confirmed that she'd woken him. The tux was long gone. In its place, he wore a low-slung pair of sweatpants and a just-crawled-out-of-bed scowl that she remembered from when they'd been a couple. She knew how to erase the scowl. Unfortunately it involved hugging and kissing and other currently inappropriate behavior. And all that inappropriate behavior wouldn't just work on his scowl. It would also work pretty well on removing the sweatpants. Too bad, too. She could use a few hugs and kisses. If only she could count on those sweatpants staying put.

Gray regarded her in disbelief. "What the hell happened to you?"

"It's a long and tragic story. Too long and tragic to go into out here." She spared a hasty glance down the hallway. A large, beefy man was striding determinedly in her direction. "Let me in. Quick."

Gray folded his arms across his chest. "Give me one good reason."

"Because if you don't security will throw me out of the hotel."

He followed her gaze down the hallway and grinned. "Give me another reason."

"I was mugged."

His humor vanished and he swore beneath his breath. Snagging her arm, he yanked her into his room and slammed the door shut. "What the hell happened?"

"Could I have a towel? I'm not just mugged, I'm soaked."

A knock sounded at the door and Gray pointed toward the bathroom. "Go shower. There's a hotel robe hanging on the back of the door you can use. I'll take care of security."

Emma didn't waste any time. Disappearing into the bathroom, she locked the door behind her, then pressed her ear to it. She heard the low rumble of voices, but couldn't make out the actual words. Whatever Gray said apparently satisfied the rent-a-cop because a minute later, the door closed again.

"Unglue your ear from the door and get in the shower. I'm going to call downstairs and see if I can order something for you to wear."

She backed away from the door. Gray knew her entirely too well. Maybe that was part of their problem. No mystery. "You can call downstairs, but I guarantee nothing will be open," she warned.

"I'll take care of it."

She had a sneaking suspicion he would, too. Hadn't she learned from personal experience how ruthless Gray could be when it came to getting his own way? Turning on the water full blast, she peeled off her clothes and dropped them to the tile floor. They lay in a dingy heap, an island of dirt-encrusted silk surrounded by an ever expanding pond of blackened water. To hell with it. She'd clean up the mess after she showered. Right now, getting washed and dried took top priority.

Climbing beneath the spray of hot water, she squirted shampoo into her hair from the small bottle of amenities provided by the hotel and scrubbed every inch of skin. Twice. She'd have gone for a third round, but Gray was waiting—impatiently, no doubt—and Emma forced herself to turn off the water. After drying herself and cleaning the mess she'd made of the bathroom, she wrapped up her dirty clothes in the discarded towels and pulled on the terry-cloth robe hanging on the back of the door. It left far too much skin exposed, not that Gray hadn't seen that plus quite a bit more. It just left her feeling far too vulnerable after everything that had occurred over the past twenty-four hours.

Exiting the bathroom, she found Gray waiting in the sitting area of his hotel suite. He opened one of the small bottles of whiskey from his minibar and poured her a glass. "I've arranged for some clothes. They should be delivered shortly, along with a snack." He handed her the liquor. "Drink up and then tell me what happened."

She didn't argue. Right now she needed something strong and potent—other than Gray, that was. Holding her nose, she downed the whiskey in a single gulp. Fire ripped a path down her throat and she choked. "I hate that stuff."

"I guess that explains why you're holding your nose."

"It's the only way I can get it down."

"Spill it, Emma. What happened? Last I saw of you, you'd changed back into your street clothes and were intent on escaping the wedding reception as fast as those sexy legs of yours would carry you."

"I wasn't escaping." She managed an indignant glare, which wasn't easy thanks to his "sexy legs" comment. "And just to clear up any lingering misconceptions, I wasn't running, either. Since I didn't have a hotel room for the night, I was attempting to spend a few quality minutes with a friend while I waited to catch a red-eye home.''

He waved that aside. ''Details. What happened after you left the restaurant?''

She shrugged. ''Raine and I only had time for a quick cup of coffee. After she left to catch her flight, I was mugged.'' She risked a quick look at Gray. If she didn't know him so well, she'd have missed his reaction. A muscle jerked in his cheek and his eyes darkened to a deeper shade of blue. Other than that, he did an excellent job of containing his reaction. ''The thief got away with my purse.''

''Why didn't you call me?''

''I didn't have your number.''

''Don't give me that. You could have gotten the number for the hotel from any number of sources and had them ring through to my room.''

She carefully set her whiskey glass on the table and faced him. ''You know why I didn't call. We're not a couple anymore.''

The muscles along his jawline tightened. ''And that means you can't ask for help when you're in trouble?''

''No, it just means that I try to take care of life's little disasters all by myself.''

''This wasn't just one of life's little disasters. This was serious. Were you hurt?'' His gaze swept over her and she suspected it took every ounce of his phenomenal self-control to keep from stripping off her robe and checking for himself. ''Do you need a doctor?''

''No, I don't need a doctor. Other than a few bruises here and there, I'm not injured.''

''How did it happen?''

She curled up in one of the overstuffed chairs in his sitting area. Exhaustion had begun to set in, enhanced by the whiskey, and she fought back a yawn. "I was in line to go through the metal detector and this nasty piece of scum did a run by."

"A run by?"

"You know. He ran toward me, grabbed my purse, and kept going." She tried a teasing smile. "There was only one problem. I was still connected to my purse."

Gray used a word that brought a flush to Emma's cheeks. "He dragged you?"

"Just a little way. I managed to get my arm unhooked from my purse before he could kick me."

"Kick you!"

"It's okay. Honest it is. He missed." Gray wouldn't like this next part. She cleared her throat. "What happened after that was probably my fault."

He swore again. "Tell me you didn't go after him."

"I went after him."

"Dammit, Emma." He thrust his hands through his hair. No doubt he'd have preferred wrapping them around her neck. "What the hell were you thinking?"

"I was so mad, I guess I wasn't thinking."

"No sh—"

"Hey! For your information, I would have caught him, except the little jerk ran outside. It was raining and my heels weren't made for running, much less running in the rain. My heel caught on a broken piece of pavement and I took a header into the nearest puddle. The thief escaped with my money, my credit cards, and my plane ticket. Oh! And my bridesmaid gown." The sudden realization that she'd lost the dress upset her more than anything else and she blinked back tears. "Oh, Gray. He got that, too. I still had it stuffed in my purse."

"Sort of like a red flag to a bull."

"I hadn't thought of that, but it's possible, I suppose." She sniffed. "Considering the state of my clothes after I went sailing across the airport floor and made that swan dive into the mud puddle, I could have used that dress, too. At least then the hotel staff wouldn't have thought I was a bag lady."

"Your clothes are the least of my concern." He hesitated. "But I am sorry you lost your bridesmaid gown. I know how much it must have meant to you."

"Thanks."

"What concerns me more is that you could have been hurt."

"I'm fine," she hastened to reassure.

"You call this—" he gestured to encompass the series of bruises and scratches decorating her arms and legs "—fine?"

She tucked her legs under the hem of the robe and tried to pull her arms, turtlelike, deeper into the roomy sleeves. "All right, so maybe fine is a slight exaggeration."

"Slight."

She brushed that aside. "The bottom line is... One of the cops took pity on me and gave me enough cash to get here." Which reminded her. "I have his address in the pocket of my slacks. I hope the rain didn't wash it away. I'd really like to send him a thank-you card when I return his money."

"I'm sure we can track him down if you lost the address. At least you had enough sense to come here." His mouth tightened. "Though you weren't going to ask me for help, were you?"

She wondered when they'd get back to that minor

detail. "I thought, under the circumstances, it might be wiser to go to Widow Bryant's room."

"Why?"

The bluntly spoken word impacted like a shot.

CHAPTER FIVE

Subject: You're dead!
To: "Screw-up Extraordinaire"
Shadoe@CupidCommittee.com>
From: Grayson_Shaw@galaxies.net

This time you've gone too far. I asked how you were going to get her to spend the night with me, but having her mugged? Mugged!?! Damn it, Shadoe, she could have been seriously hurt. She could have ended up in the hospital. The bastard tried to kick her when he grabbed her purse! You better keep out of my sight because if I get my hands on you, you're dead!

Gray

P.S. I want her stuff back. And make sure that bridesmaid gown of hers is in perfect condition or I'm going to have to kill you a second time.

"Gray—"

"Answer my question, Emma. Why did you go to Widow Bryant's room instead of coming to me when you needed help?"

Emma hesitated, not sure what she should say. The truth would leave her too vulnerable. But knowing Gray, he'd demand nothing less. "I wanted to call you."

"Right. That's why you were pounding on someone else's door."

She attempted a self-mocking smile, but couldn't quite pull it off. Not when tears threatened. She didn't dare let them fall or she'd never get through the next few hours. "You have no idea how badly I wanted to call you." Or how horrified she'd been by that knowledge.

"Then why didn't you?"

How could she explain all the reasons she'd shied from turning to him in a moment of crisis? Their parting had been devastating. She still ached for him, ached for what they'd had, as well as what they might have had if they'd been able to work out their differences. The problem was, she couldn't trust him. Not any longer. And how could they build a successful relationship without trust? But the main reason she hadn't called had been fear, pure and simple. She'd been afraid to open a door that would allow him back into her life, afraid of getting hurt again.

"It would have been so easy to call you," she admitted. "So easy to fall into your arms and let you take care of life's little problems." He started to object and she held up her hand. "Or life's big problems. I gather getting mugged qualifies as a big problem?"

"You're damned right."

"The bottom line is... I can't keep taking the easy way out, Gray."

"And I'm the easy way?"

She nodded. He might not like her answer, but it was honest. "After we broke up I realized how much I'd come to depend on you."

"You aren't alone in that." The confession seemed ripped from him. "We depended on each other."

He'd surprised her with that one. "Really? I never would have guessed."

"Why?" He paced across the sitting area. When he'd reached the far recesses of the room, he turned to confront her. "Because I'm a man? Because men are so self-reliant they don't need anyone or anything? Or is it just me you tag with those characteristics?"

He wouldn't like her answer. "You." She could tell her admission hit hard. In typical Gray fashion, he absorbed the blow without flinching, while she curled deeper into the chair, retreating from the pain. "I also realized that if I were ever going to get on with my life, I needed to learn to take care of my own problems and not count on you to help me out every time I found myself in a tight spot. Running to you has gotten to be a bad habit."

"Only because you have a knack for getting into trouble. And I have a knack for getting you out."

"Don't you think it's time I learned to get myself out of trouble?" Fine words. And yet, here she sat in hot water once again. And there stood Gray taking care of her problems, the same as he'd always done.

"I think it's in my job description. I think it's been part of my job description for a good thirty years now."

Emma shook her head. "Not any longer. I'm a changed woman, thanks to you. You're chocolate, remember? And I don't do chocolate anymore."

A rare smile split his face. "I thought I was fudge."

"That, too."

"Well, I've decided that if you eat enough fudge you'll build up an immunity to whatever problems it causes. What do you say? Shall we give it a try?"

She fought back a laugh. She didn't want to revive all the old feelings he inspired. She didn't want to share a private joke, or have him communicate with a simple look, or tumble into insanity when he touched her. Those moments were finished and she didn't dare resurrect them. To lose that sort of love once in a lifetime had just about killed her. To go through it again would finish her off.

Time for a strategic retreat.

"Good try," she acknowledged. "But that tactic isn't going to work any better than any of your others."

"Tactic."

She didn't back away from his displeasure, but fixed him with a steady gaze. "You know the word, Gray. You ought to. I think you're the one who put it in the dictionary. You don't make a move without a plan."

His mouth tightened. "We're back to that, are we?"

"Face facts. You were ruthless as a kid and you're even more ruthless now. You do whatever it takes to accomplish your goal." She grimaced. "Right now your goal seems to be to drive me insane."

A hint of laughter gleamed in his eyes, despite the seriousness of their discussion. "Is it working?"

"Far too well."

"You've always known what sort of man I am." His amusement faded. "Or you should."

"Of course I do. I still didn't expect you to turn that ruthlessness against me, or Tee, or our friends and neighbors," she protested. "I can't believe you don't understand that."

"I understand."

She could barely contain her frustration. "Then how could you steal Tee's business away from him?"

He ran a hand through his hair and she suddenly realized that he appeared as exhausted as she felt. It had been an endless day for both of them and it didn't look like it would be over anytime soon. "You told me you were worried about Tee. You told me his business had suffered some serious reversals. You told me his business was ripe for a hostile takeover. When I looked into the matter, I discovered you were right."

Didn't he get it? "But you weren't supposed to be the one to take it from him!"

"You preferred that an outsider step in?"

Her response came fast and furious. "At least then it wouldn't have felt so personal. It would have just been business."

"It was just business."

"That's your father talking."

He went perfectly still and she realized she'd made a serious error in judgment. "Don't ever compare me to my father," he warned very, very softly.

She did some hasty backpedaling. "I know you're not your father's son."

"Not even a little."

"But the way you chose to handle this—"

"Was nothing like what Paddy would have done."

"At least he'd have done it with charm," she muttered.

"Is that what you want? Charm?" He stalked closer. "Do you want me to tell you how beautiful you are? Should I flatter my way into your bed? You realize what comes after that, don't you? I saw it often enough growing up. Once you've been well bedded I'll simply slip off like a thief in the night, taking whatever valuables I can lay my hands on."

"You don't slip away." Instead, he kept coming back, wanting more.

"You damn well better remember that. You think I'm ruthless? Hell, sweetheart. Paddy could give lessons. Only he pretties it up with a few sweet words and endless discussions about how he's doing you a favor as he robs you blind. But that doesn't change what he is. My father's a con man." Emma couldn't begin to imagine how tough it was for Gray to voice that accusation. "He always has been, always will be."

"No one would ever accuse you of using Paddy's methods to get your way," she attempted to placate.

"Seems to me that's exactly what you're doing." She couldn't mistake the depth of Gray's pain. "But there's a difference. A big one. When I come after you, you can see me coming. I let you know what I want, when I want it, and how it better get delivered."

"No joke. I worked for you, remember? I have close and personal knowledge of Mr. Red-and-Black in action. The bottom line is all that counts. We don't discuss the issue. We don't debate it. And we certainly don't compromise."

"Discuss and debate?" His expression iced over. Crossing to the minibar, he opened another of the small liquor bottles and poured himself a drink. "Don't you mean, swindle and cheat?"

Swindle? Cheat? Dear heaven. How could she have known him for so many years and not made the connection? She escaped her chair to join him by the minibar. "Do you think discussing an issue is the same as conning someone?" she asked in disbelief.

"I'm not going to try to talk you around to my point of view simply to get my own way."

"Because that's like conning someone?"

"How many ways do I have to say it?" His anger seethed closer to the surface. "I'm not Paddy. I don't sweet-talk."

"So I've noticed," she said dryly. "That doesn't change the fact that it's all or nothing with you. Taking such a rigid stance prevents compromise. Compromise isn't the same thing as conning someone. It's finding a middle ground that works for both parties."

"I understand the concept of compromise."

"Do you?" Emma wasn't so sure. "In all the time I've known you it's either your way or no way. Paddy uses charm and deception to get what he wants. You simply sweep in and take it. At least with Paddy's method I'd be left with a smile on my face."

He pitched the empty glass bottle toward the trash can. It slammed against the side before ricocheting in, punctuating his displeasure. "That's because you haven't seen the path of devastation he leaves in his wake. Maybe you were too young to remember what happened to the Putnams. I don't think they were doing much smiling when they lost their farm thanks to dear old dad's get-rich-quick scam."

"You fixed that, didn't you? I remember Tee saying you stepped in and prevented them from losing everything."

"Some things can't be fixed," he replied tightly. "Their farm went, despite my efforts to save it. I guarantee, the Putnams aren't singing the praises of anyone named Shaw. Not that I blame them."

"But you tried." She shook her head. "I don't understand, Gray. You did everything within your power to help the Putnams. How could a man like that take down one of his oldest friends?"

His eyes went flat, the vibrant blue emptying of all expression. "Is that Tee's version of events?"

"You know my grandfather would defend you to the death. He's made every excuse in the book for what you did. But the bottom line is that you now own Palmer Shoes, and Tee, who used to own it, doesn't even have a job there. What makes it worse is that I'm the one who dropped it in your lap." She turned away from him. "It never occurred to me that you'd take advantage of what I'd told you in private."

"You mean in bed."

She swung around to face him again. "Yes. In bed." She fought against the threat of tears. "In a moment of weakness I confided in you. And you took advantage of my confidence. How is that different from what you accused Paddy of doing?"

"Dammit, Emma! I didn't take what I wanted and sneak away afterward. You left me, remember?"

"How could I stay after you used me to get your hands on my grandfather's business?"

He tossed back his drink and set the glass down with excessive care. "I'll explain this once and only once. Tee doesn't work at Palmer Shoes because he didn't agree with the changes I planned to implement—changes that will ultimately turn the business around. In a fit of anger, he quit. And he tried to get others to march out of there with him in one huge harebrained protest. Fortunately calmer heads prevailed before matters went too far, and no one lost their livelihood."

"Except Tee."

"The only thing keeping that old man holed up in that mausoleum he laughingly calls a home is his own foolish pride. He's welcome back at the factory whenever he wants."

"But not as the man in charge."

"No."

"You expect him to go from owner to worker?"

Gray shrugged. "Personally I don't give a damn. It's his choice. He wouldn't have been the owner for much longer regardless of whether I'd stepped in. He was fast headed toward bankruptcy."

"And you saved him from that."

He didn't respond to her sarcasm. He didn't have to. Emma had known him too long not to recognize the truth when she saw it.

She stared, appalled. "Was it really that bad?"

He delivered the news in typical Gray fashion— blunt, unvarnished, and painfully honest. "It was worse."

"Dear heaven."

"My reaction was a bit stronger."

It took Emma a minute to recover her composure. "That doesn't change the fact that you betrayed my confidence."

"And you'll never forgive me for that."

She wanted to. But there were some principles too important to compromise. "No, I can't."

"Fine. Don't forgive me. I don't need forgiveness." He straightened away from the minibar, his gaze reflecting his determination. "There's only one thing I need from you."

"What's that?" she whispered.

"Take a wild guess."

Emma moistened her lips. It didn't take a lot of guesswork, wild or otherwise, to decipher his intention. She tightened the flimsy cloth belt cinching her waist. All of a sudden she felt horribly underdressed, and she had a feeling it would only get worse before Gray was through. Somehow she had to find a way to stop him.

"You better not try anything," she warned. "Room service is on its way."

"I'm not hungry for food."

"That's funny. You look sort of hungry."

"Predatory, not hungry. There's a difference."

"Oh." She didn't need to utilize more than a half dozen brain cells to figure out what sort of prey topped his list. Something blond, brown-eyed, and wearing a terry-cloth pelt. She broke into speech. "I'm glad you're such a control freak. You never have been one to allow emotions or impulses to govern your actions. And it's a good thing, too. Otherwise, I'd be worried."

"I suggest you start worrying."

She held up her hands and backed away. "You really don't want to do anything we won't regret. And we won't regret making love even though it's wrong. Very wrong. Totally, absolutely, without question, wro—"

The final word ended in a tiny shriek as he scooped her up in his arms and deposited her onto the bed in one easy move. "You never have been very good at logic. You can't even argue your way out of my bed." He brushed a damp lock of hair away from her forehead. "Why is that, do you suppose?"

"Because secretly I want to be here." Her confession took him by surprise. It sort of took her by surprise, too. "That doesn't mean I should stay."

"I'm so tired, Emma." He whispered the words close to her mouth, his breath the sweetest of caresses across her cheekbone and temple. "I'm tired of being alone. I'm tired of fighting. And I'm tired of waiting for you to get over your anger."

"Then you shouldn't have gone after Tee's business."

"My taking control of Palmer Shoes hasn't hurt anyone. It certainly isn't a valid reason to end our relationship. Especially not now, when it's over and done."

"Don't you understand?" she protested. "It isn't your taking over the company that I object to. It's how you went about it. I won't stay with a man I can't trust."

His hand slid to the belt securing her bathrobe. "You can trust me. You've always been able to trust me."

"Maybe. At one time." She covered his hands with hers, preventing him from loosening the knot. "But that's not true any longer."

"Because you think I betrayed your confidence?"

"You *did* betray me."

"I didn't betray anything. I tried to play knight in shining armor to your damsel in distress, and save your precious town. You're the only one who doesn't realize that. Instead, I've become the villain of the piece." Pain added a heartrending roughness to his voice. "How the hell did that happen, Emma?"

"You know how it happened. You were there every step of the way."

He ended any further discussion by sealing her mouth with his and following her down onto the mattress. She started to push him away, but her brain failed to adequately communicate itself to her body. Instead of shoving at him, she encircled his neck with her arms, tugging him closer.

It wasn't fair. All he had to do was kiss her and she lost all reason. She knew—*knew*—they were wrong for each other in every possible way. Gray had always put business ahead of any other consideration. He based all his decisions on logic and reason. Emotions never factored into the equation.

But she wasn't made that way. Her decisions were based on gut instinct and what felt right at the time. And right now Gray felt incredible. She missed him. She missed him more than she thought possible. Even when she'd been so terribly hurt by his betrayal, the feelings she had for him hadn't died. Not entirely.

Her mouth parted beneath the urgency of his. Even flavored with the bitter tang of whiskey, he tasted incredible. He tugged at the belt securing her bathrobe and she murmured a reluctant objection. She should stop him now before this went any further. And she would, too, just as soon as she'd gotten her fill of this one kiss. Of course, by then it might be morning and Gray would have done a heck of a lot more than kiss her.

Her hesitation allowed him the opportunity to work the knot of her belt free and the bathrobe fell open. He didn't take immediate advantage of her vulnerability. Instead he hesitated. It was so out of character that she lay still beneath his darkened gaze.

"You're beautiful," he murmured. Reverently he brushed his thumb across the peak of her breast. The nipple pearled, responding to the familiarity of his touch. "We were made for each other, Emma. Your body recognizes that fact, even if your mind refuses to."

As though to prove his point, he fit his hands to her breasts, weighing them in his palms. His hands felt so good. They belonged on her body. They belonged anywhere and everywhere. On her face. Her breasts. Cupped between her legs until she wept for his possession. He must have read her mind because he began a tantalizing exploration, slow and thorough and intimate. Heat washed across her skin, following the path of those hands.

She loved this man. How could she have tried to convince herself otherwise? She'd loved Gray as a foolish girl when life had been all about building a tree fort and swimming in Nugget Creek and marveling over how silly boys were compared to girls. She'd fallen in love again as a hormone-rampaging teenager when the most important things in life had been hot-blue eyes, hotter sports cars, and to-die-for glimpses of the hottest bod in Palmersville. And then she'd fallen for him all over again when she'd been old enough to understand that love was more than how well various body parts interlocked, but about character and intelligence and heart.

Leaving Gray had been the most difficult decision of her life. And right now she couldn't remember why she'd been so foolish. Ruthless. It had something to do with his being ruthless. Whatever the problem, it slipped away before she could fully grasp it. Reason fled in the face of a want as raw as it was primal, an ancient compulsion impossible to ignore, let alone resist.

Gray's mouth consumed hers, biting and melding in urgent demand. His leisurely exploration had ended at the perfect place. Perfect because he was there. Perfect because she needed him there so badly. Perfect because every nerve ending in her body had congregated there waiting for his possession. She yielded to him, opened to him. It didn't matter what had happened to separate them. All that mattered right now was bringing those sensations to their ultimate conclusion. She dragged him over her, onto her, into her. To her eternal frustration, he resisted her efforts.

"We can't."

Emma fought to draw breath. "What do you mean, we can't? Have you lost your mind? You can't stop now. I'll kill you if you stop now."

"I'm not prepared."

"I'm prepared." Couldn't he tell? "Trust me, you have me fully prepared."

"Prepared prepared." He seemed to be having trouble speaking, pushing the words through gritted teeth. "Protection prepared."

She stared in stark disbelief. "You don't have—"

"No, and somehow I don't think room service would be willing to add anything to our current order. They weren't too happy with what I did request."

"Demand." She thrust a hand through her damp hair, praying the violent urges would fade sometime soon. Otherwise she might say to hell with the consequences and have her wicked way with him. "Knowing you, it was probably a demand."

"It may have been." He didn't appear terribly apologetic. Sanity was slowly returning and he flipped the edges of her robe closed. "I have a question for you."

"And I have a few words for you, too," she muttered. "None of them terribly polite."

"After what just happened, how can you think we're better off apart?"

"You know I want you, Gray. I've always wanted you. But want is just a polite way of describing sex."

"I don't accept that."

She couldn't help smiling. It was so typical of him.

"You command it, therefore it is?" Her brows drew together. "Is or isn't? You've gotten me confused."

"Isn't. I command it and therefore it *isn't* just sex." He closed his eyes, his mouth tightening in irritation. "Dammit, Emma. You drive me crazy when you go off on a tangent like that."

"I can't help it. It's the way my mind works." He manfully refrained from comment, which secretly impressed the hell out of her. Not that she'd tell him that. No point in giving him any added advantage.

"The point is," he said, "I don't simply issue commands."

"Sure you do. That sort of sweeping arrogance is ingrained in your personality. It's either one way or the other. No middle ground."

"Not that red and white crap again. Just because I think our relationship involves more than ordinary sex—"

"It's red and black. You know, debit and credit, minus and plus—"

"Crazy and sane. Yeah, I got it."

She let the crack slide, making allowances for the amount of pressure Gray must be under. "And I never said the sex was ordinary." She'd have been a bald-faced liar if she had. "But if our relationship isn't based on sex, what is it based on?"

He opened his mouth to reply when a light tapping sounded at the door. "Saved by the knock," Emma said. "My clothes, I think."

She started to roll out from beneath him, but he stopped her. "Don't go."

"It's three in the morning. I'm not going to ignore that poor man after he's gone to all the trouble of fetching me food and clothing." The knocking grew louder. "Let me up, Gray."

"It's not just sex between us," he insisted in an urgent voice. "It's never been just sex."

"Then what is it? Love?" She eyed him with regret. "I don't think so."

She could feel his tension build, the muscles cording into tight bands across his shoulders and arms as he resisted her efforts to abandon the bed. "Why not? Why can't it be love?"

She relaxed back into his embrace, relieved he'd asked a question she could actually answer. "To tell you the truth, I just figured that out today." She smoothed a hand across the breadth of his shoulders. She'd missed this. She'd missed this more than she'd have thought possible. And she'd continue to miss it when the night ended and she and Gray went their separate ways. "It was something you said earlier this evening that made me understand the problem."

"Great," he muttered. "What brilliant comment was I stupid enough to make to convince you of that?"

The knocking became a prolonged pounding. "It was the way you equate compromise with a con job."

"I never said they were the same thing," he instantly denied.

"Whether or not you're willing to admit it, I think they're identical in your mind. The problem is... Marriage involves a lot of compromise."

"It also involves love."

"True. But I don't think you could ever trust anyone enough to fully love them."

He froze. "What the hell are you talking about?"

She smiled sadly, easing out from beneath him. This time he let her go. "It's simple, Gray. The first time we didn't agree about something and I tried to reach a compromise, you'd suspect my love was just a con, that I was using love to try to manipulate you."

She didn't wait for his response. A fist thudded against the door. It was followed, if she didn't miss her guess, by a frustrated kick. She hastened to retie her robe as she traversed the room. Unlatching the various locks and bolts, she yanked open the door. "Sorry to be so long."

The delivery man didn't look happy. Nor did her apology do much to appease him. "You ordered some clothes?" He held a package in one hand and a small tray loaded with dishes in the other. He eyed her current attire in disgust. "For some reason, a bathrobe's not good enough to get you through the next few hours until the hotel store opens? You felt the need to drag half a dozen people out of bed to fix the problem?"

She took the package from him and brazened it out. "Yes. I felt an overwhelming urge to drag poor innocent people from their beds. Just for kicks."

"You also ordered a snack from our kitchen." He shoved the overloaded tray into her hands. He even had the temerity to offer a nasty grin as she attempted to juggle both package and tray. "It's normally closed now. But we were all tickled pink to get up and fix it for you."

She allowed the package to tumble to the floor in favor of keeping the tray level. "I'm delighted I could tickle so many people. Pink is a great color." She smiled sweetly. "Thanks for the food. I'm starving."

"You couldn't have been all that starving," he pointed out. "Or you would have opened the door a hell of a lot sooner. I've been knocking for at least ten minutes. It's a wonder I didn't wake up everyone on the floor."

As though to prove his point, the door directly across the hall scraped opened. No. No, no, *no!* This could not be happening. Emma attempted to slam Gray's door closed before she could be seen. She hadn't counted on the delivery man's quick reflexes.

"Oh, no you don't." He shoved his foot between the door and the jamb. "Not until you tip me, lady. And it had better be a big one because I'm not moving my foot until I've been well compensated for my trouble. Just so you know, it's gonna take a hell of a lot for me to feel adequately compensated. I suggest you start with a few Jeffersons and work up from there."

"What's all that noise?" Widow Bryant demanded. She took one look at Emma, Emma's skimpy bathrobe, and the tray of food, and her eyes widened. "Oh. Oh, my goodness."

"It's not what you think!"

"No, of course not, dear." A truly wicked smile creased the widow's face. "I wonder if Mayor Hornsby is still awake. Maybe I'll place a quick call and find out." And with that, she banged her door closed.

CHAPTER SIX

Subject: Re: You're dead!
To: "Mr. Trouble" Grayson_Shaw@galaxies.net
From: Shadoe@CupidCommittee.com
CC: "Boss Lady"
<Adelaide@CupidCommittee.com>

Gray,

Hold off killing me until I find out what happened. I'll look into the matter, personally, and get back to you. But let me assure you, we didn't arrange to have Emma mugged. At least, I'm pretty sure we didn't. Considering how many people are working to pull off this match, I suppose anything's possible. I can tell you that mugging our clients is not standard operating procedure.

Shadoe, Cupid Committee Instigator

"I STILL don't see why you have to see me home," Emma said as they pulled into Palmersville.

Gray took the complaint in stride. Not that he had much choice. She'd been grumbling ever since they left Seattle. And he'd been on the receiving end of those grumbles for that entire length of time. "You know why I'm taking you home." He flicked on the windshield wipers as the rain that had been threatening for the past hour finally let loose. "You didn't have any money, identification, or even an airline ticket. What were you planning to do? Thumb a ride?''

"Tee could have sent me what I needed."

"You'd have made him crawl from his deathbed in order to help you?" Reaching the north end of Palmersville, he turned down Tee's long, curving driveway. "That is how you described him, isn't it? On his deathbed?"

She shifted in her seat. "Deathbed might be a slight exaggeration," she admitted.

Or more than a slight exaggeration.

He parked in the circle outside the front door of the Palmer residence—a huge monstrosity of stucco and imported brick. He wasn't the least surprised when Emma bolted from the car the instant he killed the engine. She sprinted through the rain to the porch while he followed at a more leisurely pace, joining her just as she opened the front door.

He stopped her before she could escape into the house. "Forget someone?"

The question held both a challenge and a residue of unwanted hunger leftover from their encounter the previous night. She reacted instantly to both. Her chin angled to a stubborn tilt and she darted back out of her grandfather's house and onto the porch, swinging the door closed behind her. It didn't look as if she intended to let him in and he released a silent sigh. So much for doing things the easy way. Nothing ever came easy with Emma.

Gray planted his feet more firmly on her doorstep and folded his arms across his chest, silently communicating that he wouldn't be leaving anytime soon. Through no fault of his own, he possessed a rather imposing chest. Most people he knew took one look and backed off. But not Emma. She ruffled up like an outraged feline and went toe-to-toe with him.

"Thank you for seeing me home. It was very kind of you. So was rescuing me in Seattle. And feeding me." He could practically see her running through an impromptu list of appropriate postrescue exchanges. "I also appreciate your finding me something to wear. Oh, and getting me home again."

"You're welcome. Now that you've fully expressed your gratitude, perhaps I should point out that you're supposed to invite people in, not join them outside." He lifted an eyebrow. "Still intent on doing everything backward?"

"And upside down and inside out, if that's what appeals to me." Despite her bravado, concern gleamed in her golden-brown eyes. "Why do you want to come in?"

He allowed a hint of irritation to rumble through his voice. "Why the hell do you think? To see Tee. Now are you going to let me in or are you planning on standing out here and arguing with me until you're soaked through?" He didn't wait to hear her reply, but stripped off his coat and dropped it around her shoulders.

The black raincoat shrouded her from shoulder to shin and a spark of exasperation glittered in her eyes. "Why do you want to see Tee?" she demanded. To his secret amusement, she snuggled within the folds of his coat, her actions at direct odds with her irritation.

"Did you think I wouldn't after what you told me about his health?"

"I hoped you wouldn't," she muttered.

He shook his head. "Tee's my friend, Emma, despite

our differences over Palmer Shoes. I'm not going to ignore that friendship just to make you more comfortable."

"I don't expect that."

"Then why didn't you tell me sooner that he was ill? And why didn't you tell me he was asking for me? You should have contacted me weeks ago, Emma."

He'd hit a guilt button. In response, her cheeks lit up with bright color. "How did you know he was asking for you?"

"How do you think? He called and told me." He eyed her closely. "You mentioned before the wedding that he was ill. What else is there? What haven't you told me?"

"Nothing much." It was a brazen lie. But she carried it off with panache, he'd give her that. "He'll be up and whacking the furniture with his walking stick in no time. I just need to get a quick peek at his medical records to make sure—"

Gray closed in on her. Cupping her chin, he lifted her face to his. A gusty northern wind rushed by, carrying the scent of cedar and the threat of more rain. It raked Emma's hair, scattering raindrops like diamonds across the honey-colored strands. Had he been mistaken about Tee's well-being? He'd assumed the old buzzard had been sulking over Palmer Shoes. This didn't sound like sulking. This sounded serious. Maybe not deathbed serious, but bad enough.

"I want the truth, Emma. How sick is he?" The question held a terse demand, but he couldn't help that. Concern for Tee's health kept him from treading with his usual care.

Emma released her breath in a long sigh. "You know Tee," she said grudgingly. "He's doing as well as can be expected for a man who won't follow his doctor's orders.''

"Be more specific.''

The truth escaped in a rush. "He had an attack a few weeks before Tess's wedding, though the test results were inconclusive. Every other time he's taken one of his turns, he's bounced right back.''

"But not this time.''

Emma shook her head, fighting tears. "He's retired to his bed. He's been there two full weeks now.''

That stopped him. "Tee's in bed? Voluntarily?'' His mouth tightened. "You forgot to mention that part, Emma.''

"Did I?'' She retreated deeper into the folds of his raincoat. "Did I also forget to mention that Doc Crosby has washed his hands of Tee? Or that he won't see anyone except his lawyer?''

Gray swore beneath his breath. "Yes, you also forgot to mention those details. Anything else you've neglected to mention that I should know about?''

She shrugged. The quicksilver movement threatening to dislodge his coat. The rain hadn't let up and, unable to help himself, he twitched the coat back into place. "Nothing leaps to mind,'' she said. "But stay tuned. You never know what might occur to me in another hour or two.''

"Tell me about this lawyer.''

"It's been awful, Gray.'' A combination of irritation and frustration rippled through her voice. "That old shark visits every single day. After one of his longer visits, Tee suggested I get in touch with you.''

"Suggested?''

"Okay, fine. Ordered.''

He buried a smile. "I see how well you took to his suggestion."

"About as well as I take to his orders," she admitted. "Or yours, for that matter. Still, I should have phoned you. I would have, too, except—"

"Let me guess. You didn't call because of our break-up."

She didn't duck the truth. "Yes. But you're here now." She shot him an assessing glance. He was all too familiar with that expression, perhaps because he'd learned from experience that it rarely boded well for him. "And now that you are here, I suggest you come up with a game plan for resolving the situation."

Hell. He'd forced the issue. He had no one to blame but himself when she turned around and dumped the problem in his lap. He glanced upward at the bank of windows lining the second story of the massive house. Tee's room was directly overhead and the twitch of one of the curtains confirmed that someone had witnessed their arrival. "Okay. Here's my game plan."

She smiled in admiration. "That was fast."

"That's because it hasn't changed any since I first formulated it this morning. I'm going to do what Tee asked when he called."

Her admiration turned to alarm. "Tee called you? When? Why?"

"We can discuss it inside." Gray reached around her and turned the knob, shoving open the door. "Knowing your grandfather, he's already been told I'm here, so I suggest we go see him before he starts whacking the walls with that cane of his."

"Walking stick," Emma corrected automatically. "You know how he hates whenever someone calls it a cane. Though knowing you, you probably do it just to stir up trouble.''

''That's me. A stirrer of trouble.'' He made a move in the direction of the house. Thankfully, Emma fell back without protest, allowing herself to be ushered across the threshold. Right on cue, a loud thumping sounded from above. ''I believe that's our signal to join Tee.''

Gray removed his coat from around her shoulders and hung it on one of the pegs that lined the wall behind the door. A hint of something fragrant and feminine wafted from the folds. To his disgust, he caught himself inhaling the delicate scent. Deliberately, he stepped away, only to turn and confront a more serious temptation in the form of Emma, herself. But then, she'd always tempted him beyond endurance, something that didn't appear likely to change anytime soon. Did she even have a clue?

Years of practice came to his rescue and he managed to face her with his usual calm control. ''You ready?''

''First tell me about Tee's call.''

If his raincoat had been too big for her, the clothes the hotel had provided were every bit as bad. The black knit top swamped her small frame. The neckline drooped off one shoulder, while the sleeves hung from her fingertips. With an impatient exclamation, she shoved the spare material up to her elbows only to have it slide back down again.

''He rang the room before we left for the airport. You were in the shower.''

''Did he know I was with you?'' she asked.

''Yes. Widow Bryant had diligently spread the word by then.''

She spared a quick glance upward, shoving at her sleeves again. "Was he upset?"

"He said—and I quote—get your sorry backsides home and be damn quick about it."

"Oh, dear."

"Nicely put. I don't believe my reply was anywhere near that cordial." Time to get this show on the road. "Anything else I should know before we go upstairs?"

She nodded. "Maybe I should warn you that he mentioned calling in a favor."

It didn't take Gray a moment's thought. "No problem. Whatever he wants, it's his."

Emma looked intrigued. "Don't you want to know what the favor is first?"

"I don't need to."

And he didn't. Gray owed Tee far more than he could ever repay, despite their falling-out over Palmer Shoes. During a time when his home life had been sheer hell, Tee had opened the doors to his home and had shown by example how a real father behaved. Every life lesson Gray held dear came courtesy of Tee. Still, Gray didn't like the sound of this mysterious favor anymore than he liked the sound of endless meetings with a lawyer. Thomas T. Palmer despised lawyers almost as much as he despised asking for help. It didn't make sense that he'd request either one unless there was serious need.

Gray inclined his head toward the stairs. "Come on. Let's get this over with."

Emma caught his arm before he'd taken more than a single step. "Wait."

"What is it?" The mild words belied the painful demand rippling beneath the surface.

Oblivious to his reaction, she moistened her lips, revealing an uncharacteristic hesitancy. "Does he know about…us? The first us, I mean."

That captured his attention. "The first us?"

"The 'us' before Widow Bryant blabbed. The 'us' Tee wasn't supposed to know about. The 'us' that had an affair. Have you said anything?"

"Tee and I are still friends, aren't we?"

"Meaning?"

He didn't immediately answer and her hands tightened on him. He stared at them for an endless moment. Unable to help himself, he caught hold of her. Sliding his hand along her cheek, he contented himself with simply tucking a wind-ruffled lock of hair behind one ear. Did she have any idea how tightly he held himself in check? She couldn't or she'd have put as many barriers between them as physically possible.

"Meaning that if Tee seriously thought I'd had you in my bed, he wouldn't be asking to see me. He'd have ripped me apart long ago and scattered my carcass to the four winds."

She didn't back away from his touch. Instead she leaned into it and a smile briefly quivered at the corners of her mouth. His control slipped a notch and his fingers sank deeper into her hair.

"Somehow I doubt Tee could have done serious damage," Emma insisted. "You're more than a match for him."

"I would be if I chose to fight him."

"Are you saying you wouldn't?"

He slid his thumb across the arching curve of her cheekbone. He shouldn't give in to the temptation to touch her. But right now he couldn't seem to help himself. It had been a long, grueling day and he'd take his compensation anywhere he could get it. "I'm saying that I would have deserved whatever punishment he saw fit to dish out.''

A hint of shock tarnished the gold of her eyes. "Because you slept with me?"

"Because we didn't marry after I took advantage of you. I let you escape."

She frowned at his phrasing. "As I recall, we took advantage of each other."

"Tee wouldn't have looked at it that way."

"And," she continued as though he hadn't interrupted. "You couldn't have kept me from leaving."

He didn't bother replying. Nothing he said at this point would make any difference. He carefully adjusted the neckline of her shirt before releasing her. "Tee's not the most patient of men. We'd better get upstairs before he sends out a search party."

She planted herself in front of the steps. "You couldn't have kept me from leaving," she repeated. "The choice was mine."

Gray held on to his temper through an act of sheer will. "There are always ways to tie a person down. It was your choice to go and my choice to let you go. I suggest we leave it at that."

He didn't give her the opportunity to argue. Easing her to one side, he started up the steps. After a momentary hesitation, she chased after him, catching up at the first landing. "This discussion isn't over," she warned.

He climbed without pause. "Somehow I didn't think so." Crossing the hallway to Tee's bedroom door, he rapped once. "Fair warning, Emma. Don't bring Tee into the middle of this."

Pain swept across her expressive features. "I

wouldn't do that. Not to Tee. And whether you believe me or not, I wouldn't do that to you, either.''

He'd clearly hurt her with his comment. Before Gray could respond, a testy voice issued from behind the door, practically rattling the frame. "What the devil are you two waiting for? Get your tails in here!"

Gray lifted an eyebrow. Interesting. That didn't sound like a man on the verge of death. Curious to discover what was going on, Gray opened the door and walked into the spacious master suite. The drapes were drawn, only a hint of dim light relieving the oppressive darkness. A woman stood by the windows, while Tee occupied the four-poster bed, propped up against a half dozen pillows. A faint trace of cigar smoke lingered in the air.

Interesting didn't begin to characterize the situation. Suspicious, seemed a more accurate description.

"What's going on Tee?" Gray demanded.

"Didn't my granddaughter tell you?" The old man paused for dramatic effect. "I'm dying."

"Don't say that—" Emma began.

Tee waved aside the protest with an impatient hand. "Face facts, girl. I'm a goner. Why the hell do you think I've had my lawyer visiting every day. Or why I asked for Shaw?"

"I understand it's because I owe you," Gray inserted smoothly.

"That's right." Tee's dark eyes glittered from the depths of his bed. "And I intend to collect before I kick off."

"What, precisely, do you plan to collect?"

"Nothing much." Tee smiled without humor. "Just a marriage proposal."

"Grandfather—" Emma broke in.

"Relax, sweetheart. I'll handle this." Gray's mouth twitched. "Okay, Tee. Would you marry me?"

"Not me, you jackass." Tee whacked his walking stick against one of the sturdy oak posters. The entire bed shuddered beneath the impact, but both stick and poster held. "Have you no respect for the dying?"

"Easy, Mr. Palmer." The woman standing in front of the window crossed to the bed with a rustle of starched authority. "We mustn't excite ourselves."

Gray fought back a bark of laughter. "And you are?" he managed to ask politely.

"You may call me Nurse Jones." She made a production of checking Tee's pulse. "I'm here to take care of Mr. Palmer."

"Of course. You'd have thought the uniform would have clued me in."

"Perhaps a program would help?" she murmured. "That way you can keep track of all the various players in our little production."

"What's going on, Grandfather?" Emma questioned sharply.

"It's simple. I want Gray to propose to you. It's my dying wish to see the two of you married." He folded his arms across his chest. "There. I've said it. Now all that's left is for you to get down to business."

Gray hooked a finger beneath Emma's chin and re-hinged her jaw so she could close her mouth. "Congratulations, Tee. You've left her speechless."

She glanced wildly from one to the other. "This isn't funny!"

"I didn't leave her speechless for long," Tee groused.

"It takes practice, but it can be done." Gray frowned

at his one-time friend and mentor. "What's really going on, Tee? What's this all about?"

"It's about an old man squatting square on death's doorstep. An old man who wants to see his poor, innocent granddaughter safely wed before the Grim Reaper drags him to his doom."

"Over the top," Nurse Jones offered in an aside.

Tee winced. "Hell. I never was much good at subtlety."

"I'm not marrying Gray," Emma announced, turning a defiant gaze in his direction.

"Funny," he shot back. "I don't recall asking."

"At least, not today."

Tee's walking stick went into action again. "Quiet!" he ordered. "I'm serious about this. I want you two settled before I die."

Emma approached the bed, perching on the edge. "You're not going to die." She gathered his gnarled hand between both of hers. "I want you to stop saying you are."

"Everybody goes sometime. I can't last forever, Emma, despite what I thought. Before I go, I want to know that you're happy and settled."

An element of sincerity underscored his words and Emma teared up in response. "Why?" she whispered. "Why is it so important that I be happy and settled with Gray? Why not happy and settled by myself?"

"You know damn well why. You and Gray have been playing house behind my back." He released her hand and flicked a finger across her cheek. "You ought to blush, missy. I raised you better than that."

She broke into hasty speech just as she used to as a child when she'd been caught out. "It was all a misunderstanding. The hotel gave away my room. That's why I was with Gray in Seattle.''

"I'm not talking about Widow Bryant catching you last night. I'm talking about those months you worked for Gray. You were living with him then, weren't you?''

She looked stricken. "You know about that?''

"I may be old, but I'm not stupid." Tee stabbed his cane in Gray's direction. "He took advantage of you. Now I want the boy to do right by you.''

"That's not necessary. We pretty much took advantage of each other.''

Tee's face fell into stubborn lines. "It is necessary, regardless of who did the advantage taking. He stole my business away from me. He's not going to steal your reputation, too.''

Emma's features assumed an expression identical to her grandfather's. "I appreciate your concern. But people don't marry simply because their reputations have been compromised. Not anymore.''

"They do in Palmersville. And they do when it's my granddaughter." He turned to Gray. "Will you salvage her reputation or are you going to take that from me, too?''

"I'd be happy to marry Emma," Gray answered promptly. "Unfortunately she won't have me.''

"That's the first sensible decision she's ever made," Tee muttered.

Emma folded her arms across her chest, her sleeves dangling off her fingertips. "If it's sensible, then why are you pushing me to do it?''

"Because people are talking. Worse they're placing bets. I won't have it, Emma. I won't have people talking about you that way.''

"Idle gossip bothers you, but having me marry a man I don't trust is acceptable?"

Tee shifted beneath his covers. "Aw, hell, girl," he muttered. "You can trust Gray."

"Even after what he did to you?"

"That has nothing to do with you."

"It does when I'm the one who gave him the information he needed to take away Palmer Shoes. He's the most ruthless man I've ever met."

"Only when it comes to business."

She glanced at Gray and the expression in her eyes ate at him. He wasn't only ruthless when it came to business. He was just as ruthless in his personal life. The manner in which he was attempting to win Emma proved that. He frowned as he mulled over some of the accusations she'd flung in his direction over the past two days.

Maybe he was a bit red and black about things. He'd never given it much thought until now. Sure, he had a tendency to pursue his goals with unswerving determination. Hell, relentless tenacity worked or he wouldn't use it. But what other way was there? Forty-eight hours ago he'd have claimed there wasn't any. Standing here now, meeting Emma's gaze, he had the uneasy feeling he'd better find one.

"Please, Emma," Tee urged. "Do this for me."

An odd emotion flickered in her eyes, one that caused Gray to flinch. He opened his mouth to interrupt, but Emma spoke first.

"Okay, Grandfather. If that's what you want, that's what I'll do. I'll marry Gray." Without another word, she stood and left the room.

Tee swore beneath his breath. "Well, don't just stand there, boy. Go after her."

For some reason Gray couldn't get his legs to move. Why had she stared at him like that, like he'd committed a crime against nature? And why, when he should be feeling an intense satisfaction, did he feel like every nerve in his body had just gone to red alert. "What more do you want from her?" The demand held a gritty quality. "She agreed to marry me, didn't she?"

"And you believed her?" Tee snorted in disgust. "She said yes, but that look in her eye says not a chance in hell. Go after her and convince her to stick by her promise."

"How do you suggest I do that?"

"How should I know? You're the ruthless one. Threaten her. Trick her. Get down on your knees and beg her. I don't care what it takes. Just do it."

"Maybe you should tell her how you feel," Nurse Jones suggested. "I assume you do have feelings. Or is that just an ugly rumor?"

Gray crossed to the door. "I think it's time I handle this without so much help, thanks, all the same."

"Yeah, that'll work," came Tee's closing volley. "Look how well you've done up till now."

Gray closed the door behind him and deliberately stood there for a minute. Opening the door again, he poked his head inside. "You might want to pull that cigar out from under the covers before you set your bed on fire." He glanced toward the nurse. "Adelaide. Always a pleasure. Great disguise, by the way. Emma didn't have a clue."

She patted her iron-gray wig. "It's a knack."

"Give my best to Tom, Dick, and Harry. And you can tell Tom I still plan to kill him."

With that, he gently shut the door again.

* * *

Tee yanked his smoldering cigar from beneath the covers and glanced at Adelaide. "Tom, Dick, and Harry?" he questioned the instant the door closed for the second time.

"My children. Dick and Gray were at university together."

"Hell." He jabbed his walking stick at the bedpost. Heaven help anyone who dared refer to it as a cane. Canes were for doddering old men. A walking stick was for—he grimaced—for vain old men who didn't use canes. "Then the boy knows this is a setup."

"I believe Grayson figured that out the minute he stepped foot in the room. Emma would have figured it out, as well, if we'd spent more time together at the wedding. Fortunately for us she was more preoccupied with Gray than the mother of the groom."

"I can't believe it," Tee exploded.

Adelaide lifted an eyebrow. "What can't you believe?"

"I'm feeling guilty. Me! Tom T. Palmer. The man who'd do whatever it takes to get his own way is developing a conscience." He glared at the stub of his cigar. "Who'd have thought it? It's downright disgraceful."

"You can always suffer a miraculous recovery."

"And I would suffer, too." He escaped his bed and crossed to his dresser, rummaging around until he found his gold lighter. "If I let Emma off the hook she'd slip away slicker than greased lightning."

"Then you either suffer the pangs of righteousness. Or you allow your better nature to take advantage of your granddaughter and force her to marry the man she's spent the past decade madly in love with."

He released a bark of laughter. "That's what I love

about you, Addie. You're a woman of keen vision and unscrupulous determination.''

"We do make a pair, don't we?"

"Damned right. Okay, you win." He relit his cigar. "If I sit here and think about it long enough all those wishy-washy impulses will fade right away. Now that I ponder the matter, I can't imagine what got into me. Never went soft like that before."

"Don't you worry. I'm here to make sure it doesn't happen again." She offered a devilish smile. "I never go soft."

CHAPTER SEVEN

Subject: Enough!
To: Gray Shaw <Grayson_Shaw@galaxies.net>
From: "Boss Lady"
<Adelaide@CupidCommittee.com>
CC: "Thomas T. Palmer"
<teepalmer@worldstar.com>
"Mr. Not-at-all Extraordinaire"
<Shadoe@CupidCommittee.com>
"Tess Lonigan" <tlonigan01@altruistics.net>
"Mayor Hornsby" <thebigcheese@worldstar.com>

I have had quite enough. As of today, I am taking over the match between Grayson Shaw and Emma Palmer. There will be no further interference from any outside parties or this short romance will come to a fast end. Any questions are to be directed to me and no one else.

Adelaide, President and CEO, Cupid Committee

P.S. There better not be any questions.

GRAY caught up with Emma at the top of the steps. She'd looked so odd right before accepting his marriage proposal. Hurt. The sort of hurt that had cut to the bone. It stirred something inside of him, disturbing him more than he cared to admit. He studied her expression, relieved to see that she appeared more temperate now.

119

"We need to talk," he said.

"I agree." She started down the staircase ahead of him. "We have a serious problem to discuss."

Her black skirt—also provided courtesy of the hotel—billowed out around her trim calves. Huge red poppies covered the skirt, winking saucily with each determined step. What was it with her and red, anyway? If he didn't know for a fact that the hotel had selected her outfit, he'd swear she taunted him with the color. Gray followed behind, doing his damnedest to avoid the fluttering poppies. Reaching the bottom of the steps, she headed into the library, turning the instant he stepped foot over the threshold.

"Okay, I've agreed to marry you." She planted her hands on her hips. "Now what do you plan to do about it?"

Great. An easy question for a change. "I plan to marry you."

Easy question, wrong answer. "Oh, no," she instantly retorted. "I agreed to marry you to satisfy Tee. But it's not going to happen."

The hell it wasn't. Business instincts, honed during more adversarial crises than he cared to recall, came on line. If she thought he'd been ruthless before, it was nothing compared to what was to come. "Why don't we return upstairs and explain that to your grandfather?"

"That won't be necessary."

"Somehow, I didn't think it would be." The crack was probably not his smartest negotiating tactic.

She bristled at the comment. "You got us into this mess. That superanalytical brain of yours can darn well get us out again."

"Sure. No problem."

Something in his tone must have clued her in to his real feelings. She stared in disbelief. "You're not going to do anything, are you?"

"No."

"I can't believe this!" She began pacing. The poppies stopped winking and began to snap and snarl. "Why would you marry me when we don't have anything in common?"

Wasn't that obvious? "Because it's what we both want. And deep down, I think you know that. You're just not ready to admit it."

"You're wrong."

"Am I?" He approached, allowing all he felt and believed about her to reflect in his eyes and voice and stance. "Am I wrong?"

She held up her hand. "Stop right there."

"What's the matter now?"

"You're not using—" she flipped her dangling sleeve at him to indicate everything from his head to his toes "—all that to influence me. Keep your distance until we settle this."

He suppressed a smile. Whether she was willing to acknowledge it or not, they were meant for each other, despite his bride-to-be taking the longest possible route to arrive at that conclusion. He took a single step backward. "Is this far enough?"

"No. But I guess it'll have to do." Her brow crinkled in thought. "Where was I?"

"Keeping our distance."

"Before that."

"Something about us being perfect for each other."

"Exactly!" She scowled at him. "I'm glad you recognize it, too. We're not the least bit perfect for each other. We already can't agree on anything. Do you think that's going to change over time? We'll be at each other's throats within a month. A month? Hah! What am I thinking? I give it a day.''

''Bull.'' The field of angry poppies distracted him and he shifted his gaze upward. Unfortunately her knit top wasn't much better. Despite being a nice restful shade of black, it continued to droop off her shoulder, exposing far too much soft, creamy skin for his peace of mind. All he could think about was having her tumbled across his sheets, wrapping herself around him in the most exquisite of embraces. ''We were together for six full months and it worked great.''

''Until you stole Tee's business.''

He sighed. ''Yeah. Right up until then.''

''Don't you see? That's my point. Everything was fine until you turned into Mr. Ruthless. What makes you think it won't happen again? Because the second it does, I'm out of there.''

''I guarantee it'll happen again.'' Steel crept into his voice. ''In fact, it's going to happen right now. And you'll learn to deal with it during our marriage the same as you'll deal with it now. You're not helpless, Emma. Far from it. You've always been perfectly capable of standing up to me.''

She stopped her pacing and the poppies fell silent. ''Why do I get the feeling I'm not going to like this next part?''

''You're going to like it just fine. Negotiating's fun.''

''Negotiating,'' she repeated. ''Not compromising, but negotiating. Because heaven knows, you don't compromise. That's a con job, as I recall.''

"That was your interpretation. Personally I haven't taken a definitive stance on the subject of compromise. Should I let you know once I've reached a decision?" He didn't bother to wait for a response. Why give her the opportunity to blister his hide any more than she already had? "On the other hand, I consider negotiation a vital business practice and as far removed from a con job as it's possible to get."

She let that slide. "What are we negotiating?"

He leaned against Tee's desk and folded his arms across his chest, more comfortable now that he was following his own agenda, instead of hers. "I haven't made any secret of the fact that I want to marry you."

She waved that aside, her sleeve once again flapping off the ends of her fingertips. "I'm well aware that for some odd reason I'm on your current to-do list." She struggled to free her hand from the excess material so she could tick off on her fingers. "Steal Tee's firm. Wreck Tess's wedding. Ruin Emma's reputation. Marry the poor, ruined woman."

He chuckled. "Quite a list." Crossing to her side, he gathered up the excess material hanging off her arm. A few expert twists and he had it neatly knotted at her elbow. "For your information," he explained, repeating the procedure with the opposite arm, "marrying the poor, ruined woman tops the list."

"Lucky me." She inspected her sleeves with reluctant admiration. "How do you do that?"

"It was a university class I took. 'Disarming techniques for ruthless entrepreneurs 101.'"

The pun provoked a quick laugh. "Disarming?"

"You'll be pleased to know I aced the class." Emboldened by his success with her sleeve, he hitched up the neckline of her shirt. Disarming techniques apparently didn't work with necklines. Her top slid down the slope of her shoulder once again and he left it there. A little torture was good for the soul. "What do you say we get down to some more of those ruthless techniques I learned? Do you want to open the negotiations, or shall I?"

"You're joking."

"Not even a little." He took marriage to Emma very, very seriously. "You've accused me of only seeing things in black or red. How about this for a little black and red. What will it take to convince you to marry me? What's your bottom line?"

She stared at him, shock intensifying the gold of her eyes. "I can't believe you're asking me that."

"You're the one who's always faulting me for being ruthless. Why the surprise when I live up to my nature?"

"You can't negotiate your way into a marriage."

"Watch me."

Her shock faded, rapidly replaced by a glare of outrage. "Forget it. I'm not for sale."

"And I'm not buying." Years of practice kept him focused on his ultimate goal, instead of how much he stood to lose if he failed to negotiate an agreement. Why worry about failure? His mouth compressed. He was only risking his entire future. "But there must be something you want that only I can give you. Something that will convince you that our marriage has a chance for success."

She started to reply, then paused. "Something only you can give me," she repeated.

He didn't dare allow himself to believe he'd found

a weakness. "Name it and it's yours." It took every ounce of control to make the offer in a calm, steady voice.

"Anything I ask, you'll do?"

"If it's within my power." *Please let it be within my power.*

"You're serious about this, aren't you?"

"Dead serious."

"You want to marry me that badly?"

"I want to marry you that badly."

Their gazes locked as endless seconds ticked by. He had no idea what she saw there or what she hoped to see. But he didn't back down from that look. He returned it full measure.

To his astonishment, she capitulated. "Okay. There are two things I want from you."

He regarded her warily. Her agreement had been too easily won. Either her requests were impossible to fulfill, or she had another plan for ending their engagement, and these requests were a delaying tactic. "And if I give you those two things, you'll marry me?"

"Yes."

"Name them and they're yours, but it has to be something I'm capable of doing."

"Oh, you're capable of doing these things."

Gray could read between the lines. He was capable...he just wouldn't like them. He released his breath in a silent sigh. It didn't matter what she asked of him. He'd do it. He'd do anything for Emma, even if there weren't so much at stake. Didn't she know that? "What's first?" he asked.

"First, I want Tee reinstated as president and CEO of Palmer Shoes."

Aw, hell. The poppies began to dance again, their glee setting his teeth on edge. What he wouldn't give for a weed whacker right about now. "You're going to regret asking for that."

"No, I won't." The expression in her eyes was painful to observe. An intense love for her grandfather vied with a bone-deep anger directed squarely at Gray. "Tee's in that bed because you stole the company his father founded, a business that literally created this town. Worse, he's lost face with the people of Palmersville. For a man as proud as Tee, that's a fate worse than death. No wonder he's given up on life."

"He's faking."

She turned on him, her fury almost knocking the poppies off her skirt. "How dare you suggest such a thing! That poor man is sitting at death's door, and it's all your fault." Gray had been an idiot to rescue her hand from the arm-eating sleeve. Now she was free to plow a finger into his chest to emphasize her point, something she did with painful relentlessness. "And you're going to fix that by giving him back Palmer Shoes."

"Even if it means the company going down? Even if it means that two-thirds of the people of Palmersville will lose their jobs if the old man screws up?"

"That won't happen."

There was no point in explaining that Tee's return to the helm of Palmer Shoes guaranteed the business going under. Facts and figures weren't going to win against blind emotion. "And your other demand?"

An intense longing flickered across her face, disappearing before he could react to it. "I'll marry you if you can find out what I truly want and give it to me."

He stared blankly. "Come again?"

"You heard me."

He'd heard. He just hadn't understood. "Okay... What do you want?"

"I'm not telling. You have to figure it out." She wrapped her arms around her waist. It was a telling gesture, one that spoke of loneliness and estrangement. She was holding him at a distance and he didn't like it. Not considering their current topic of conversation. "If you give me what I want, I'll marry you."

For some reason, he was having trouble wrapping his brain around her final request. "Let me get this straight. You want me to figure out some secret desire. I'm supposed to guess what it is and fulfill it."

That odd look returned, more intense this time. A yearning for...*what?* "It would be nice if you didn't have to guess. I'd rather you understood what I wanted."

Dammit! He'd been so close. All she'd had to do was give him a couple of tasks—he didn't care how difficult—and like a fairy-tale prince of old, he'd overcome any obstacle and face any danger to fulfill them. But a secret wish? "How the hell am I supposed to figure out what you want?" He thrust a hand through his hair. "Knowing you, whatever it is will change on an hourly basis."

"Not this." Something about her expression warned that she took this particular demand very seriously. "I'll tell Reverend Franklin what my second condition is. That way you can be sure that I won't change it on a whim or in order to get out of our agreement."

Gray scrambled to set parameters, to bring some sense of organization to help counterbalance Emma's brand of chaos. "When am I supposed to give you this second thing? During the ceremony?"

She shook her head. "Before might be best. That way we don't have to waste our time preparing for a wedding that's not going to happen."

Comprehension dawned. "You don't think I can figure out what it is, do you?"

To his concern, her mouth trembled. "No," she whispered.

There was only one way to convince her. He drew her into his arms. This time she didn't resist. Forking his fingers deep into her hair, he tilted her face up to his. The loose waves spilled across her bared shoulders in delightful abandon. That sort of abandonment was one of the reasons he loved her so much. Where he planned every detail, life simply happened to Emma. Where he graphed and charted and enumerated, she embraced life, chasing wherever it led. His was a world of red and black, while she was a butterfly, carrying every color of the rainbow on her wings.

He lowered his head and kissed her. With a joyous moan, she wrapped her arms around his neck, giving herself up to the moment. He deepened the kiss, feasting on her mouth. With that one kiss he told her in every way possible what she meant to him. They belonged together. They always had. And nothing, not even a secret desire, would keep them apart. Reluctantly he pulled back.

"I don't consider anything about our engagement and wedding to be a waste of time," he said. "This is real. This is going to happen and I want you to enjoy every minute of it. When we get to the front of that church, I'll give you your second request. Guaranteed."

"How can you be so sure?" she asked in wonder.

He answered with absolute honesty. "Because there isn't a man alive who knows what you want better than me."

Gray thrust open Tee's bedroom door. "Okay, what the hell does Emma want?"

"Oh, it's you." Tee yanked his cigar out from beneath his bedcovers. Chomping down on his stogie, he held the sheet up to the light, tisking over the round burn hole he found there. "Thought it might be my granddaughter. Should have known better since she'd have been polite enough to knock before barging in here."

"You haven't answered my question, old man. What does she want?"

"Who, Emma?"

Gray clamped his teeth together, wishing it was in his nature to throw temper tantrums or smash innocent furniture or break his fist punching holes in walls. "No, you old buzzard. Nurse Jones."

"How the hell should I know what she wants?" he asked in an aggrieved voice. "It's not like she's a real nurse or anything. No telling what sort of predilections she has. She's down in the kitchen grabbing a bite to eat. Go down and ask her your own self if you're so all-fired interested."

"If you weren't in that bed, I'd beat you to a bloody pulp."

Tee chuckled. "Aw, don't get your skivvies in a twist. I'm just yankin' your chain, boy. Now, what's your problem?"

"Emma is my problem. Emma has always been my problem."

Tee nodded morosely. "Yeah, she has that effect on

a lot of people. Endearing in an annoying sort of way.''

Gray took up a stance by the window and stared out at the expanse of neatly trimmed lawn and overflowing flower beds visible from this wing of the house. ''You'll be pleased to know that she agreed to marry me.''

''You did it? You really did it?'' Tee jumped from his bed and sketched a quick jig, using his walking stick for a partner. A thick wreath of smoke circled his head like a tarnished halo. ''Knew that deathbed scene would get to her.''

Gray turned around and thrust his fists into his pockets. ''Don't get too excited. She has conditions.''

''Aw, hell.'' The jig came to an abrupt end. ''What conditions?''

''First off, she wants you reinstated as president and CEO of Palmer Shoes.''

Tee offered a sharklike grin. ''Now ain't that sweet. My little grandbaby is defending her grandpappy against the mean ol' corporate pirate.''

''You think it's sweet? Dangerous, is more like it.''

Tee waved that aside. ''Relax. I don't want the job.''

''Well, you're stuck with it whether you want it or not. It's one of Emma's conditions, and by heaven, I'm going to fulfill it.'' He ground to a stop. ''And what the hell do you mean you don't want it? After that stunt you pulled with the protest, now you're telling me you don't want the job?''

Tee had the grace to look embarrassed. ''That was my pride doing my thinking.''

''It could be worse, I suppose,'' Gray muttered. ''Pride isn't what does the thinking for most men. That's usually reserved for other parts of their anatomy.''

Tee chuckled. "You speaking from personal experience, boy?"

"Never mind which part of me does what." Gray paused long enough to marshal his thoughts. Now that he had Tee alone and in a reasonable frame of mind, it was past time they straightened out their differences. "Emma's under the impression that you're holed up in this bedroom at death's door because I took Palmer Shoes away from you."

"I have to admit that I was a might peeved with you about the takeover. At first." He let out a long stream of smoke. "But the longer I sat in this bed, the longer I thought about it. And thought and stewed and thought some more. And all that thinking brought me smack up against a rather interesting conclusion."

"Which was?"

"I was sittin' plumb in the middle of a 'can't lose' proposition."

Gray grunted an agreement. "I wondered when that would occur to you."

"You have nobody to blame but yourself that it took me so long to figure it out." Tee's jaw assumed an aggressive slant. "You're the brain around here. You should have explained it to me. If you had, you'd have saved yourself a few headaches."

"As I recall, you weren't exactly willing to listen to anything I had to say," Gray pointed out. "Not then."

"I might have been a bit hot under the collar." His aggression faded and for the first time in all the years Gray had known him, Tee looked his age. "Then I realized that I wasn't responsible for the fate of Palmer Shoes, anymore. The pressure was off, thanks to you."

"You're welcome." Gray's irony provoked a commiserative smile.

"Hell, boy. I really do appreciate what you're trying to do. The business has been sliding down a slippery slope for a full decade now. In the past year, that slide's turned into a free fall. If you hadn't stepped in, we would have gone under."

"Try telling that to Emma."

"Not a chance. I'm perched in the catbird seat and I'm not budging. If you screw up, I can point the finger and say, 'it's all his fault.' And if you turn things around, I can claim it was dumb luck. With the shares of the company I still own, I'll be laughing all the way to the bank. Why would I want to screw with that by going back to work?"

"Because it's the only way I'll get Emma to marry me. That's why."

Tee made a face. "Damn."

"Listen, all you have to do is show up for a few months. Then you can tell her it's too much stress and you've decided to retire."

"She won't buy it."

Gray didn't cut him any slack. "Convince her."

"Okay, fine. I'll convince her." He shot Gray a mischievous look. "I convinced her I was dying, didn't I?"

"You sure did. And as soon as I have her safely married, I'm going to beat you to a bloody pulp over that one, too. She's been worried sick about you."

"If it gets you two back together, it'll be worth it. Nothing else I said or did worked." Tee shook his head in disgust. "Lord love her, but she's a stubborn girl."

"I can't imagine where she gets it from," Gray said dryly. "So if you're not up here sulking over Palmer Shoes, then why are you here?"

"Simple. I'm under orders from Addie."

Gray cut loose with one of his more colorful expressions. Why hadn't it occurred to him sooner? He'd assumed Adelaide was posing as a nurse as a result of his request. Apparently he hadn't been the only one who'd appeared before the committee. "Let me guess. You went to the Cupid Committee."

Tee lifted an eyebrow. "Familiar with them, are you?"

"You might say that."

"Don't tell me you—" Tee released a crow of laughter. "You went to them, too? Adelaide told me you were a friend of her son, but she neglected to mention the part about you being another client. Heaven save us from devious women. They'll be the death of us, yet."

"If you breathe one word about this to Emma, you really will be at death's door." Gray's curiosity got the better of him. "What happened when you went?"

"They asked me to help out." He looked entirely too pleased with himself over that minor detail. "Didn't think I'd be of much use until Adelaide said they needed someone underhanded, nefarious, and totally reprehensible. Then I knew I was the perfect person for the job."

"Sounds like Adelaide. What did she want you to do?"

"Can't you guess? I was supposed to die." Tee used his walking stick as a golf club and lobbed a shoe across the room. It smacked the far wall and dropped neatly into his trash can. "Or come as close as possible."

"Why?" As if he didn't know.

"Deathbed requests carry a lot of weight with people." He scowled at Gray. "They'd have to in order to convince Emma to marry you."

Damn. "She never had a chance, did she?"

"Nope. One way or another, the good folks of this town intend to see their favorite daughter married to their favorite son." He eyed Gray's grim expression. "What's the matter now?"

"Aside from a small matter of dishonesty?"

"Right. Aside from that."

"Emma's second condition."

Tee's snowy eyebrows pulled together. "You never did mention what that was."

"It's simple. She asked me to give her what she truly wants."

"Which is?"

"That's just it. She won't say."

Tee stared, nonplused, his cigar dangling from the corner of his mouth. "Come again?"

"You heard right, old man. She wants something from me. But she's not admitting what it is. I'm supposed to guess."

"Guess."

Gray paced the full length of the room. "Do I need to tell you I'm no good at guessing? Facts, figures, logical analysis. No problem. But guessing..." He shook his head.

"Now, calm down, son. This isn't a problem," Tee insisted. "We can do this. Have you told her you love her, yet?"

Gray stared blankly. "Sure. I guess."

Tee chuckled. "Baloney. You haven't, have you?"

"I tried to. She said love was a con job or some such thing. I hate to be the one to tell you this, but your granddaughter doesn't always make sense. She does a lot of talking, but her ideas aren't very logical.''

"Gets that from her grandma." Tee lined up a half dozen pairs of shoes and went back to lobbing them into his trash can. "Now listen up. This is gonna be a snap. You'll see. All you have to do is tell her you love her at the appropriate moment and you two will be wedded and bedded within the week. I guarantee.''

"And if that's not it?''

"Hmm." Tee paused to consider that unpleasant possibility. "Then you better have a heavy-duty pair of galoshes, boy. Because you're standing a shovel short in hip-deep bullsh—''

"Been there before. Hoped to avoid going back.''

Tee nodded gloomily. "Most men do. But when it comes to women, we all wind up in it at one point or another.''

"Tell me something I don't know.''

Tee stabbed the glowing end of his cigar in Gray's direction. "If you don't figure out what Emma wants, you're going to lose her.''

CHAPTER EIGHT

Subject: Git going!
To: "Boss Lady"
<Adelaide@CupidCommittee.com>
"Grandson-in-law-to-be"
<Grayson_Shaw@galaxies.net>
"Head Instigator"
<Shadoe@CupidCommittee.com>
"Tess Lonigan" <tlonigan01@altruistics.net>
"Hornsby Hornblower"
<thebigcheese@worldstar.com>
From: "Thomas T. Palmer"
<teepalmer@worldstar.com>

All right, people. I've done my part. I pulled off what none of the rest of you incompetent cupids were capable of doing. You can all thank me for getting Emma and Gray engaged. Time for the rest of you to get your backsides in gear so we can see them safely hitched! I want great grandchildren and I want them nine months from the wedding day and not a day later. (Or sooner, for that matter.) Now git going!

T.

"I DON'T know what the rush is," Emma complained. "We've been engaged all of, what? An entire hour?"

"Two."

"Fine. Two hours." Gray opened the door of the bridal salon and she walked in ahead of him. "We have

136

plenty of time to pick out a gown and whatever else we'll need for the wedding."

He thrust his hand into his pocket, fisting it around the contents. "Time is the one thing we don't have." There was an implacable hardness about him that worried her. She knew that look from the months she'd worked for him. He got it whenever he'd fixed his sights on a goal. Once fixated, he became unwavering in his quest, pursuing what he wanted with relentless determination. "I'm not taking the chance that you might change your mind. We're getting married in two weeks and that's final."

She stopped dead in her tracks. "Two weeks? That's impossible."

"Difficult, yes." He shepherded her further into the store. "Not impossible."

"There's no way we can pull off a wedding in that amount of time."

"Watch me."

"I don't want to watch you." Flowers, a gown, the church, invitations. Tess and Raine! Would they even be able to come? The logistics were staggering. "I'd prefer a long engagement. Say…six months or so."

"Two weeks." He looked around the shop. "Where is everyone? The place is deserted."

"Didn't you see the sign in the window? Mary Lou had an errand to run." Emma returned to her main topic of concern. "About our engagement. I'm serious. I think long and cautious is best."

"Try short and sweet." He glanced at her, lifting an eyebrow. "Or were you hoping for long in order to find a way out of our marriage?"

"No." Definitely.

He walked to the window to examine the sign. "It

says she'll be back in fifteen minutes. We're supposed
to make ourselves comfortable until she returns.''

"Gray—"

He didn't give her a chance to argue. "Forget it,
honey. I'm not changing my mind. Nor will I debate
the issue. You only had two requests when you agreed
to marry me and neither of them had anything to do
with when.''

He had a point. "In that case, I'd like to negotiate
a third request.''

Amusement turned his eyes a startling shade of blue.
"I'm sure you would. Maybe this will perk you up.
The sooner we marry, the less time I'll have to figure
out your second request.''

For some reason his comment had the opposite effect. Instead of feeling relieved, a coldness washed over
her. She knew what caused it. She'd been hiding from
the truth for months now. She wanted Gray to meet
her demands, wanted it more desperately than she'd
have thought possible. And there was only one reason
why she'd feel that way—because, deep down, she still
loved him and wanted to marry him. She closed her
eyes. How could this have happened? She thought she
was over him.

Fortunately Gray's attention was centered on the
racks of dresses scattered around the showroom floor
and he missed her reaction. "Why don't I start at one
end and you start at the other and we'll meet in the
middle,'' he suggested. "If we're systematic about it
we can have a gown picked out by the time Mary Lou
returns.''

Emma fought to sound calm. Normal. Casual, even.
"Don't be ridiculous. Mary Lou said to make ourselves
comfortable, and that's what I intend to do.'' Spying a

tea service tucked into a corner of the room, she headed for it. "Would you like some coffee?"

"I'd rather get down to business. We came here to pick out a wedding dress, remember?" He removed his hand from his pocket and plucked one off the rack. "How about this?"

"Forget it. I'd look like a giant doily."

He stared blankly. "A doily."

"You know. One of those lacy things grandmothers put under stuff."

"Lacy things."

Emma filled a delicate porcelain cup with freshly brewed coffee and carried it to the sitting area. Setting her saucer on the coffee table in front of the couch, she lifted a vase of flowers resting in the middle and pointed to the tatted circle she found beneath. "A doily."

"Right."

"Now picture a stack of them five feet high. Then picture it hollowed out with me shoved in the middle."

He winced. "Got it. No doily dresses." He thrust aside a few more gowns and held up another. "What about this one?"

"All those crisscrossy straps make me think of an accident victim covered in bandages." She collapsed onto the couch. "This is pointless, Gray. You might as well have a cup of coffee because I'm not going to pick out bridal gowns with you."

"Why not?"

"For one excellent reason. The groom isn't supposed to see the dress before the wedding. It's bad luck. And we don't need to tempt the fates to send us any more bad luck than we already have. When Mary Lou returns, I'll tell her what I'm looking for and set up an appointment and a fitting schedule. Will that do?"

"Sure, fine." He crossed to join her. Checking his pocket before he sat down, he started to pull something out, then clearly changed his mind. "After we've talked to Mary Lou I thought we'd head over to the florist."

"What do you keep playing with in your pocket?" she asked.

His brows snapped together. "Nothing."

His reaction instantly roused her curiosity. "It's not nothing. You never play with things in your pocket. But you've been doing it ever since we left Tee's. What is it?"

"I'll show you later."

"It's not like I'm doing anything right now," she pointed out. "What's the big mystery? Show me."

He hesitated for a moment, then shoved his hand into his pocket and removed a small jeweler's box. "I was going to wait until tonight." A rough quality entered his voice. "Take you someplace romantic when I gave this to you."

She stared, frozen. "Is that what I think it is?"

He snapped open the lid of the box. A diamond sparkled from deep within the velvet bed. Carefully he removed it and took her hand in his. "This is for you," he murmured and slid the ring onto her finger.

It hurt to breathe. "It looks familiar."

"That's because it's your grandmother's wedding band braided with your mother's engagement ring. Tee gave them to me."

Gray couldn't possibly have had this done in just a few hours. It would have been impossible to accomplish even if he'd had a few days. A job of this magnitude would have required weeks. She stared at the ring, scarcely able to take it in. The workmanship was stunning. She'd always loved the tiny circle of diamonds that had made up her grandmother's band. She'd considered it elegant and feminine. Now, gracefully interwoven with her mother's gold-banded solitaire, it was breathtaking.

"When?" She couldn't manage more than that one word, but Gray seemed to understand what she was asking.

"Six months ago. I was going to ask you to marry me then." His mouth twisted. "I never quite got around to it."

Because he'd taken over her grandfather's company and she'd left him because of it. "I don't know what to say." Tears gathered in her eyes. "It's beautiful. Thank you."

"You'll wear it?"

They'd have to rip it from her finger to stop her. She lifted her hands to his face, sliding them along his jawline. Shards of brilliant light broke from the diamond's surface, splintering like tiny stars across his angled features. "Yes, Gray," she assured him, a tear slipping free. "I'll wear it."

And then she kissed him, revealing in that kiss all that she'd kept hidden in her heart. She loved this man. She'd always loved this man. Unfortunately love wasn't always enough. Another tear escaped. He could negotiate an engagement and place his ring on her finger, but the end result wouldn't be a marriage. How could it?

He'd never meet her second condition. Not the Grayson Shaw she knew.

Time slipped quickly by, gathering speed with each passing day. Gray kept her busy running from florist to bakery to reception hall. The amount of energy he put into the preparations was overwhelming. At first, she thought he pushed so hard to keep her too busy to protest their marriage. But after a week had swept by, she realized that wasn't it at all.

He was enjoying himself. He took an active interest in everything about their wedding, right down to the selection of the flowers, teasing her when she couldn't choose among the vast array. It didn't seem to matter how large or small the detail, he participated, offering his opinion, but never overshadowing her preferences. They were special moments. Joyous moments. Moments she'd never forget.

She'd also never seen him so relaxed—except for those few instances when they were alone. Then she could feel the heightened awareness simmering just beneath the surface and sense how tightly he held himself in check. Time would slow and intensify, as if they hovered on the brink of some great discovery. It was during those brief times that their engagement actually seemed real, as though the possibility existed that everything would work out and they'd spend their lives together.

The morning before the wedding Emma managed to sneak away from all the last minute confusion, determined to enjoy a few minutes alone to relax and catch her breath. Not that she had much opportunity to do that. No sooner had she settled into Tee's chair when a light knock sounded at the door.

Gray poked his head into the room. "Good. I found you."

"Is there a problem?" Not that there had been any so far. With Gray, there were only solutions.

"Actually I have a present for you."

She perked up at that. "What did you get me?" she demanded, rubbing her hands together in anticipation.

"Not what. Who." He pushed the door wide-open and stepped back. Tess and Raine walked in, grinning from ear to ear. "You missed out on spending the day with them before Tess's wedding. I wanted to try to make up for that."

Emma stared in disbelief. In so many ways Gray proved how much he cared. First the wedding gown, then that incredible engagement ring, followed by all the endless wedding details. And now this. With the exception of the ring, this was the best gift he'd given her so far, something that showed an innate understanding of her needs. A tender light gleamed in his eyes, one that silently communicated all they didn't dare express aloud. Escaping her chair, she flew aross the room, straight into his arms. Then she did the only thing possible for a woman in her situation. She burst into tears.

"What do you mean Emma's missing?" Gray demanded.

Tee scowled. "Something wrong with your ears, boy? Or do you just have trouble understanding plain English? I said...Emma's gone missing. What part of that don't you get?"

Gray held on to his temper through sheer willpower. Better the fiery heat of anger than the bitter coldness tying his gut in knots. "When did you last see her?"

"One minute she was in the library, laughing and joking with her two friends. The next they're kissing everyone goodnight. What is it with those women, anyway? All huggy, kissy, huggy." He swiped a gnarled hand across his cheekbone. "I'm a poor, old man, just recently escaped from my deathbed. My heart can only take so much excitement."

"Tee!"

"I'm gettin' there, boy. Don't get your britches in an uproar." Beneath his bluster, Gray could sense a nervous concern. And if Tee was worried... "The second all that kissy stuff was over with, Emma ran out the door."

"With Raine and Tess, or on her own?"

Tee's fist tightened around the burled knob of his walking stick. "All by her lonesome. Bridal jitters would be my guess. Can't think of any other reason she'd be leaking like a rusty faucet."

"She was *crying?*"

Tee gave the floor a good thumping with his walking stick. "Isn't that what I just said? The girl sprung a leak something fierce." He glared at Gray. "I warned you bringing her friends into this was a bad idea. They probably spent the whole night talking her out of marrying you."

"And did they?" Gray asked evenly.

"Maybe," Tee confessed. "A little."

"And you know that...how?"

"Can't help it if the good Lord graced me with keen hearing," he muttered.

"Mmm." Gray refused to cut him any slack. "Along with an unscrupulous nature and a pair of ears that undoubtedly spent the entire evening glued to the wall closest to the library."

Tee snorted. "A fat lot you know. There's a vent in the kitchen that links direct to the library. Can hear every word that's uttered in there. Course, you have to stand on the table to do it."

Gray shut his eyes, the control on his temper growing more tenuous by the moment. "Let me guess. You just happened to be in the kitchen for the better part of the evening, standing on a table."

"Can I help it if I got hungry? Or if I decided to test how sturdy the kitchen table is?" His expression turned crafty. "I can tell you that table was good and sturdy. Got something else to tell you, too. Something that'll make you a happy man."

"First things first. I need to find Emma." Nothing was more important than that. "If you'd round up a flashlight, I think I know where she might have gone."

"The tree fort?"

"That would be my guess."

After checking to make sure the flashlight had fresh batteries, Gray headed out the back of Tee's house. A late summer moon had just slipped above the horizon. Fat, sassy, and full of itself, it hung low in the nighttime sky burnishing the landscape with such silvery radiance, it made the flashlight unnecessary. He didn't bother turning it on until he hit the woods that led down to Nugget Creek.

The old path had become seriously overgrown in the past several years and Gray could guess why. Not enough kids came through here. A shame, since this place had been a special haven when he and Emma had been young. Maybe it would be again. All he had to do was convince his tearful bride-to-be that Palmersville was the perfect place to raise a passel of kids, every last one of them bent on turning their old tree fort into the bridge of the Starship Enterprise. At least, that's what it had been when he and Emma had played there.

The trail petered out a short distance from the river. A huge oak marked the end of the path, its magnificent branches encompassing the distance from the edge of Nugget Creek to a good twenty feet into the woods. Nestled in the crook of one of its boughs was a large fort that he, Tee, and Emma had constructed in another lifetime. To his surprise, it had been maintained in tip-top condition over the years, the structure showing signs of fresh lumber and nails. Now who had put so much time and care into a tree fort? Tee, or Emma? If he were a betting man, he'd peg Emma as responsible.

Swinging up the rungs of the ladder that had been nailed to the trunk, he climbed to the base of the fort. "Permission to come aboard, Captain," he called.

To his relief, a watery chuckle escaped from overhead. "What's the password, Matey?"

"Beam me up, Scotty."

A rumbled head appeared above the ladder. "That's not the password."

"Damn."

"That's not it, either."

"Live long and prosper?"

"Nope."

"Make it so? Engage?" How the hell was he supposed to remember the stupid thing after more than a decade? "Use the force, Luke?"

"You're mixing your movies," she explained kindly. "The force is *Star Wars*. I preferred *Star Trek*."

"That isn't helping me remember the password. I don't suppose you'd care to give me a hint?"

"It's 'the trouble with tribbles.'"

More than a hint, but at this point he'd take anything he could get. "Of course. I don't know how I could have forgotten the tribbles. Whatever the hell they are," he added beneath his breath. He climbed up another rung. "Are you going to let me come aboard, even though I didn't get the password right?"

"I suppose." She backed away from the opening in

the floorboards. "But my phaser's set on stun until I have a chance to check out your credentials."

"Fair enough."

He hoisted himself into the tree fort. Emma sat curled in the darkest corner, her arms wrapped around her bent knees. The flashlight seemed an unfair intrusion and he snapped it off.

"Thanks," she murmured.

"No problem."

She fell silent and Gray could sense the barriers she'd erected to hold him at a distance. Not a good sign. This wasn't going to be easy. A soft wind stirred the leaves surrounding them, the sound they made brushing against each other like quiet whispers, every one of which urging him to proceed with caution. Not that he needed the reminder. When it came to Emma, he always used the utmost care.

"So…" He scrambled for an innocuous conversational gambit. "How long has it been since we were last here?"

"Together?" The moon had crept a little higher in the sky, the light just enough for him to make out her shrug. "About ten years."

The way she'd answered snagged his attention. "And how long has it been since you were last here?"

"Six months."

Aw, hell. It didn't take a mathematical genius to run the numbers on that one. "About the time we split up?"

"About then," she concurred.

He took the next logical step in assessing the problem. "I guess that means that if you're here, something's wrong." And someone was to blame. Like him. "What is it? Didn't you have a good time with Raine and Tess? Did I make a mistake having them come?"

She buried her face against her knees. "It was a wonderful thing to do. Thank you."

He scrambled for another possibility. "Did they say something that upset you?"

"Tess is so happy with Shayde." The words were muffled against her denim-covered knees, but he caught them. Just. "You should see them together."

"And?" he prompted.

"I'm not sure we'll end up as happy as they are." The confession was filled with heartbreak and she lifted her head to look at him. The moonlight glinted off tiny silver tracks running from cheek to chin. Hell. No question what those were. Tears. "I'm not sure we'll ever work out our problems."

A muscle jerked along his jaw. "You don't think I'm going to figure out what you want, do you?"

"No." The simple reply held a wealth of pain. "If you have to figure it out, then it's not going to happen. Either you understand what I want or you don't. And I'm afraid you don't."

He scrambled for a solution. Any solution other than the one that made the most sense. Unfortunately he couldn't come up with anything. "We can call off the wedding." The suggestion was the most difficult he'd ever made. "We can wait until you're positive we should get married."

"Waiting won't change anything."

Frustration ate at him. "Explain that to me. It's beyond me why we have to go through all this business with requests and conditions. Why the games?"

She jerked as though stung. "This isn't a game. There's something I want from you. That I need from you. I have to know that you see things the same way I do. Because if you don't, our marriage isn't going to work."

"So why don't you simply tell me what you want?"

She shook her head. "I can't," she whispered.

"You mean, you won't."

"I could," she flashed back. "I could beat it into your head. But I'd rather it slip into your heart."

He climbed to his feet and paced to the side of the tree fort overlooking the river. Moonlight and shadow danced across the water, offering both clarity and concealment. It was a perfect reflection of his current situation. "You're throwing up roadblocks, Emma. And you're throwing them up because you're afraid to love me. Afraid that someday I might leave you the way your parents and your grandmother did and that you'll get hurt again."

"I'm not afraid of loving you or getting married," she instantly denied. "This has nothing to do with my parents or my grandmother."

"No?" The scepticism was clear in his voice. "Then what are you afraid of?"

"I'm afraid that when the moment comes and we're standing in front of the altar, that you won't be able to give me what I want and the marriage won't go through."

"If you say 'hell, yes, I'll take this man,' then the marriage will go through," he argued logically. "It's that simple."

"I believe Reverend Franklin prefers we say 'I do' rather than 'hell, yes.'"

A rough laugh broke free. "Honey, 'I do' doesn't begin to express how I feel about making you my wife. That's why I find this so frustrating."

"You don't have a clue what I want, do you?"

A clue? No, he didn't. But he could tell her what he'd like to do about her request, and that was to put an end to it. He wanted to drag her in front of a minister and speak whatever words it took to legally bind them together as husband and wife. Loving words that would keep her happy and by his side for the rest of their lives. Ancient vows that had been spoken throughout history. A permanent joining that they both wanted more than anything else on this earth.

He attempted to ease the tension with humor. "Does this request have anything to do with tribbles?"

"I'm afraid not. Tribbles work as passwords, but not as secret desires." She stood and joined him at the railing, standing close enough that the sweetness of her perfume eclipsed the more prosaic scents of the night. "You want a hint, don't you?"

He released his breath in a long sigh. "Are you asking, or offering? Because that sounds an awful lot like an offer."

"It might have been," she admitted.

The possibility of a hint tempted him beyond endurance, mainly because there wasn't a doubt in his mind that he could wring more than a hint from her. It would be so easy to get her to tell him what she wanted. She was vulnerable. She was emotional. And she sounded desperate. He didn't need years of training in business negotiation to know that the right few words combined with a subtle amount of pressure would get him what he needed—enough of an idea to figure out her second request.

But even as he opened his mouth to accept her offer, he flashed back on the way she'd stared at him in her grandfather's bedroom when Tee had pressured her into accepting his marriage proposal. There had been such a strange expression in her eyes, as though he'd hurt her in some visceral way. As though he'd either done or said something reprehensible, or failed to do or say something vital. He'd never seen her look that way before.

It hadn't been a surface pain, either. No, this had gone deep. Whatever had upset her that day cut to the very core of who and what she was. It had been as though the light had been snuffed from her spirit. And it had been driving him insane ever since.

Calling himself every name in the book, he shook his head. "No, Emma. No hints. We're going to do this right. When we get married it's going to be because we both feel certain that it's the right thing to do."

"Are you sure you don't want a hint?" Her fingers brushed his arm in a light, questioning touch. "Not even a tiny one?"

He fisted his hands around the railing instead of putting them on her. "No, I'm not sure. But it's how we're going to do it."

She shouldn't have touched him. It took every ounce of willpower to keep from returning that touch, from changing it into something more indelible. From wrapping his arms around her and taking her on the dusty boards beneath their feet. The urge to make her his in the most primitive way possible burned in his heart and blood and soul. He struggled to formulate a coherent thought, to bring clarity and reason to a passion fast raging out of control.

Deliberately he moved from the railing. A light wind stirred between them, helping to cool his desire. "But I need you to do something for me," he finally said. "I need you to convince me that you're not trying to stop our marriage out of fear."

CHAPTER NINE

Subject: I'm ending it
To: "Boss Lady"
<Adelaide@CupidCommittee.com>
From: "Gray Shaw"
<Grayson_Shaw@galaxies.net>
CC: "Tomas T. Palmer"
<teepalmer@worldstar.com>
"Mr. Screw-up Extraordinaire"
<Shadoe@CupidCommittee.com>
"Tess Lonigan" <tlonigan01@altruistics.net>
"Mayor Hornsby"
<thebigcheese@worldstar.com>

This is formal notification that I'm putting an end to this business. There will be no further matchmaking attempts made. All bets are officially off. No more.

Gray

Subject: Re: I'm ending it
To: Gray Shaw <Grayson_Shaw@galaxies.net>
From: "Boss Lady"
<Adelaide@CupidCommittee.com>

Gray,

Please understand that some events, once put in motion, are impossible to stop.

Adelaide, President and CEO, Cupid Committee

Subject: Re: I'm ending it
To: "Boss Lady" <Adelaide@CupidCommittee.com>
From: "Gray Shaw" <Grayson_Shaw@galaxies.net>

Impossible to stop? Watch me.

    G.

"Do you think I'm afraid to love you?" Emma asked.

Gray chose his words with care. "I think you've experienced a lot of loss in your life. Your parents. Your grandmother. To a certain extent, your friends. Hell, I'm even responsible for Tee losing his business."

"What's your point?"

"My point is that as a result of all that loss, you're afraid to love. You're afraid that if you lost someone you cared deeply about, you'd lose part of yourself." Unable to resist, he returned to her side. "Is that how you'd feel, honey? If something happened to part us again, would you feel like you'd lose part of yourself? Because that's how I'd feel."

She bowed her head. "Yes," she whispered.

"Then—"

"That's not why I put that condition on our marriage." She lifted her head again and took a step closer. "It's not because of fear of loss, but fear over our differences."

He suppressed a groan. "Let me guess. The word 'ruthless' is coming into this conversation sometime soon."

"Right about now, as a matter of fact," she admitted without apology.

"Okay, fine. I'm ruthless. Why should that keep us

from getting married? And what does it have to do with this request of yours?"

"If I came out and told you what I want, then it's just your head knowing. You'd tackle the problem like a business strategy, attacking it systematically, intellectually."

She'd totally lost him. What other way was there to overcome an obstacle? "I gather that's not how I'm supposed to resolve this particular problem."

She shook her head. "To grant my wish, you need to use your heart. If you can do that, you'll understand what I want right down to the core of your being." Her voice faltered momentarily before strengthening. "But I don't think you're capable of giving it to me, because you'd never allow yourself to think with your heart. It goes against your nature."

"Do I even need to explain how irrational that is? How do you think with your heart?"

The moonlight cut a swath across the top half of her face, intensifying the gold glittering within her eyes. "I suggest you figure that out. You can't approach this like you do a business problem, Gray. I'm not a column of numbers that you can add up and arrive at a bottom line that will resolve this. This isn't a business deal that you can ruthless your way through. Relationships don't work like that." She shrugged. "Or at least, they shouldn't."

"Dammit, Emma." He smacked the railing with his palm. It vibrated slightly, but held firm beneath the assault. "I'm not like you. I warned you that I can't change my nature. I don't approach problems heart first, like you."

"No, you attack them head-on."

"And you're telling me I can't do that with whatever

this is you want. You've tied my hands, Emma. There's no way I can win. You have me jumping through hoops for no good reason, other than to prove that our personalities are different.''

"Not just different. It's like we're two opposing species. You're a Romulan and I'm an ordinary human. What I want isn't in your vocabulary. We're totally opposite and never the two shall mate.''

"Can't I be Vulcan, instead?'' he asked in an attempt to ease the tension. "I've always been able to identify with Mr. Spock.''

A reluctant laugh escaped. "Fine. Be a Vulcan. The logic of what I'm saying should appeal to you. There's a reason species don't crossbreed. They're too different. It's not personalities or cultures, alone. It goes right down to their DNA…just like us.''

"You're saying we're so incompatible that our marriage will never survive?'' No way. "You're wrong. Somehow, someway, I'm going to prove it to you.''

"Mr. Ruthless in action.''

"Wrong. Mr. Desperate in action.'' Unable to fight his more basic urges any longer, he approached and pulled her into his arms. She didn't resist, as he half expected. She went to him as though she belonged, contradicting with her touch all that she'd just finished arguing with such passion.

She smelled of a heady combination of honeysuckle and roses, a clean fresh fragrance unique to her. It was a scent he always associated with Emma. He hadn't realized until she'd left how he'd carried that scent with him through the years. It was the same way he'd carried the sound of her voice, and the joy of her laughter.

Images of her lived with him, as well. Images of her radiant with passion and replete with satisfaction.

Images of her in celebration and pain, tenderness and irritation. He'd always assumed those images would one day grow to include their children and their grandchildren. That as Emma's hair grayed and her beauty ripened with age, he'd have decades of memories to share with her.

And he would, too. She thought he was ruthless before? That was nothing compared to what he'd be now. No matter what it took, he'd give her what she wanted. Because the alternative—losing her—was too terrible to contemplate.

"This won't be our last night together," he vowed. "Tomorrow we'll be husband and wife. I promise."

He didn't give her time to argue. He found her mouth in the darkness, kissed her with a passion she couldn't mistake. She didn't resist, but her cheeks remained damp with tears. And he knew that even though she hadn't denied what he'd said, she didn't believe him, either. He could sense her fear, feel it in the urgency of her touch and the desperation of her kisses.

"Make love to me," she pleaded.

"Why? Why tonight?"

"You know why." The words were spoken so softly, he almost didn't catch them.

There wasn't any question what she meant. "Because you're afraid there won't be a tomorrow for us."

"Do we have to analyze it?" she asked. "Can't we just have this one night without any recriminations afterward?"

Anger flared. "You mean without any recriminations when we fail to get married tomorrow? One night just for the hell of it?"

"That's up to you." Her arms tightened around his neck. "You haven't given up, have you?"

He couldn't stay angry with her. Not tonight of all nights. "I'll never give up on you."

And he wouldn't.

He kissed her again, their mouths colliding. Her lips parted beneath his, allowing him to discover the delicious heat within and he explored the sweet interior with a thoroughness designed to please. Part of him wanted to slow down, to savor every moment. Another, stronger urge, demanded he move faster, harder.

A soft moan escaped from her mouth to his. "You taste good," she told him. "Better than good."

"So do you, sweetheart." He hadn't planned to take their lovemaking far, only a few kisses. But he found himself fumbling with the buttons of her shirt, releasing one after another. The cotton edges fell open and he slipped his hands inside.

Emma caught hold of his wrists. "Wait."

"Don't stop me." The words that escaped were low and guttural, heavy with desire. "Not now."

"I wasn't going to stop you."

Stepping back, she shrugged free of her shirt, allowing it to drop to the planks beneath them. There was something simple and elemental about what she did. Something generous. An offer of her body, that surpassed a simple sexual act and became a gift of heart and soul. Her breasts were covered by a scrap of transparent silk, and she slipped her fingers beneath the straps and eased them downward, shedding her bra the same way she had her shirt. Then she reached for the snap of her jeans, the sound of the zipper renting the stillness of the night. She stripped away the final few pieces of clothing, leaving herself totally open and vulnerable to him.

Beneath the silvered moon, time ground to a halt.

Gray's breathing grew labored, the intake and exhalation loud in the quiet night air. For a long moment they stood, staring at each other. Somehow her eyes had gathered up the starlight, reflecting back the heavenly radiance. Overhead, moonbeams pierced the canopy of leaves, streams of silver filtering earthward, melting over the pale swells of her breasts and down to her belly. It stopped short of the apex of her thighs, the shadows creeping upward to shield her.

"Gray, please." She held out her hand and her diamond captured the moonlight, bursting into rainbow-colored flames. "Make love to me."

He could hear her want and responded to the heat and energy flowing from her. It only took a moment to discard his clothing. Then, he reached for her. Ever so slowly he tasted everywhere the moon led, anointing her with his tongue as he savored each hillock and valley. Then he chased the shadows, seeking out all the darkness tried to conceal from him. Her pulse pounded beneath his hands, hot and fierce. And her soft gasps filled his ears even as her taste filled his mouth.

He lowered her to the floor of the tree fort. It didn't matter that their bed was clothing-strewn planks or that they hadn't taken the proper precautions. Nothing mattered other than the overpowering forces urging them to join. To mate. To lose themselves in a desperate need as old as time. She opened herself to him, angling her hips upward to mesh with his. He tried to slow down, but the moment was too powerful to slow.

He plunged into her, losing himself in an exquisite mix of fiery heat and fluid softness. Had it only been six months since he'd last held her, made love to her? It seemed an eternity. She twisted frantically beneath him, incoherent in her need. And he did everything within his power to satisfy that need, driven by a compulsion that went beyond easy expression.

She wrapped herself around him, called to him in her siren's voice. Control was impossible. Not now. Not ever. The fire grew, a rampaging conflagration that swept them along. They burned together, burst into flames together, melded into one. Then, when it became almost too painful to bear, they found that moment of ultimate completion. He felt Emma come apart in his arms and he drove home, allowing his release to crash down on him. And in that instant of oneness, their eyes met and he knew he'd do anything—*anything*—to make her his wife.

"I swear to you this isn't the end," he vowed. "It's just the beginning."

The moon shone directly overhead, bathing them in its balmy silver light. Gray dropped a kiss on top of Emma's head. *Wipe that stupid grin off your face!* he ordered himself. But he couldn't help it. After what they had just shared, there wasn't any question in his mind that he could pull off her second request. These last few hours were a new beginning. A timeless moment of sweetness. A prelude to success. They were meant for each other, and he'd do whatever necessary to make certain that what was meant to be actually occurred. He just had to figure out what she wanted.

Not that it would be a problem. She'd claimed he'd need to use his heart, but that was simply because she approached everything that way. Heart first. That was Emma. It didn't mean he couldn't use his head to analyze the situation logically. Of course he could. He'd be sensible. Reasonable. Rational. That was how he would tackle the problem. He frowned. He'd approach

it the exact way Emma said not to. Unbidden, a touch
of uncertainty sprang to life.

He *could* do this...right?

The moon shone directly overhead, bathing them in its
balmy silver light. Emma dropped a kiss on Gray's
chest. *Don't cry!* she ordered herself. But she couldn't
help it. After what they'd just shared, there wasn't any
question in her mind that he couldn't possibly pull off
her second request. These last few hours were a final
goodbye. A timeless moment of sweetness. A prelude
to disaster. No matter how much she'd hoped they were
meant for each other, what was meant to be didn't always occur. He'd never understand what she wanted.

And that hurt. She'd warned him he'd need to use
his heart, but how could he when he'd never used his
heart to resolve a problem before in his life? Headfirst.
That was Gray. Knowing him, he'd try to use his vast
intellect to analyze the situation logically. Or...would
he? Maybe this once he'd be intuitive. Impulsive.
Caring. Perhaps that was how he'd tackle the problem.
A smile quivered at the corners of her mouth. He'd
approach it the exact way she'd said to. Unbidden, a
touch of optimism sprang to life.

He *could* do this...right?

Gray gritted his teeth, his tension building. Now that
he'd had time to mull everything over, heaven only
knew what insane request she'd come up with. Logic
didn't always work with Emma. Now that he thought
about it, it *never* worked with her. How many times
had he fully expected her to go one way and she'd
ended up headed in the exact opposite direction? His
brows pulled together. Aw, hell. This wasn't going to

work, was it? No question. Now that he'd had a chance to reconsider, there wasn't a doubt in his mind that when the time came, he'd get it wrong. Totally wrong. His hands folded into fists. Dammit! What was he going to do now?

Because no matter what he'd told Emma, he was positive he'd never pull this off. When the sun set on them at the end of tomorrow, he and Emma would be going their separate ways. Guaranteed.

Emma sighed, relaxing. Now that she'd had time to mull everything over, it was possible Gray would come up with a flash of insight. He could get in touch with his emotions. Now that she thought about it, he'd *always* had feelings for her. How many times had she fully expected him to go one way and he'd surprised her by heading in the same direction she was going? Her smile grew. This could actually work, couldn't it? Absolutely. Now that she'd had a chance to reconsider, there wasn't a doubt in her mind that when the time came he'd get it right. Exactly right. Her fists unfolded, her fingers splaying across his chest. Thank heaven. She didn't have to worry about what he was going to do.

Because no matter what she'd told Gray, she was positive he'd pull this off. When the sun set on them at the end of tomorrow, she and Gray would be husband and wife. Guaranteed.

In just a few short hours their wedding would begin and Emma couldn't wait. It really would be a new beginning, just as Gray had promised.

A new beginning? Hah! It was the end of the road as far as he was concerned. Gray thrust a hand through his hair, rumbling the waves he'd just finished taming into order. Time was up and he was about to go down in flames. And he was going down dressed in a monkey suit, no less.

Shayde and Shadoe had taken off to line up for the processional, leaving Gray with a few minutes to himself. He gave his appearance a final once-over in the mirror and grimaced. Not perfect, but it would have to do. Despite his preference for something a bit blacker, Emma had insisted that the color of his morning suit match his name. It had seemed a small price to pay at the time, especially when he considered the loving expression on her face and the excitement gleaming in her eyes. For that brief moment, their engagement hadn't been the result of some committee's manipulation. It had been real.

His expression fell into determined lines. And it would be again. Whatever it took, he'd turn fantasy into reality. Deep down, he knew she loved him, that she wanted to marry him as much as he wanted to marry her. All he had to do was get past this one small roadblock she'd set in his path. His mouth tightened. And no matter what it took, he *would* get past it. Taking a last, cursory look in the mirror, he released his breath in a sigh.

At least the damn thing wasn't red.

The door leading to the chancel eased open and Tee slipped in, doing a ridiculous imitation of a man tiptoeing into his house after a late night of carousing. The fact that he needed to use his cane to keep from falling over, made it all the more peculiar. He peered around the room, and then shut the door and locked it.

Gray fought back a laugh. "Come to wish me luck?" he asked.

"You don't need luck." Tee stabbed his stick in Gray's direction. "What you need is a little help before you embarrass yourself in front of Emma and the entire town of Palmersville."

"I don't have time for this, old man."

"Oh, yes, you do. I tried to tell you this last night, but you took off before I had the chance."

"I needed to find Emma."

Tee grabbed hold of Gray's arm. "Right now, you need to listen to me, boy, and listen good. That is, if you want to walk back out of this church with a bride clinging to your arm." He leaned closer, lowering his voice. "When Emma and her friends were having their little hen party, I overheard something very interesting…something that's gonna make you a happily married man."

"Nervous?" Raine asked.

Emma shook her head. What she felt went beyond nervousness. She didn't know whether to laugh or cry, though tears seemed a stronger possibility. Where had her earlier confidence gone? Vanished with the night, apparently. "A bride shouldn't feel like this," she said, half to herself. "A bride should be happy on her wedding day."

Tess approached, carefully settling a veil on the back of Emma's head. "What upsets you more?" she asked, pinning the gossamer tulle in place. "The fact that he might not fulfill your request…or that he will."

"I want to marry Gray. I love him more than life itself." The confession was as simple as it was painfully honest. She bowed her head. "But maybe he's right. Maybe I'm forcing him to jump through hoops out of fear."

Tess wrapped an arm around her shoulders. "What are you afraid of, sweetheart? Can you explain it to us?"

Emma struggled to put her feelings into words, to articulate what it had taken her years to understand. "Gray's my other half. He always has been. The two of us have been dancing around that fact for an entire decade, both of us a bit gun-shy because of our backgrounds." Emma plucked a tissue from a nearby box and dabbed at her eyes. "I think I've held him at a distance for so long because I knew that if I ever committed to him, if I ever allowed myself to fully love him, I'd be vulnerable. It was safer to keep those feelings at bay, to pretend they didn't exist."

"And now that you've allowed yourself to love him?" Tess asked gently.

"I can't bear the thought of losing him," she confessed.

Her two friends exchanged glances. "You don't have to go through with your second condition," Raine suggested, ever practical. "If he guesses baby booties, just say, right you are. Aren't you a clever man? You've kept him on pins and needles about whether or not you'd go through with the wedding these past few days. That should make him behave himself for…oh…at least a week."

Tess snorted. "I give it a day, tops. Mr. Ruthless won't stay down for long."

"Sometimes ruthlessness is a good quality," Emma offered tentatively.

"Sure it is," Raine agreed. "It's been a vital personality trait in every man I've ever known who's been, say, a corporate raider, a repo man, a tax auditor, or a cowboy."

Emma blinked at that. "A cowboy?"

Raine scowled. "You'd understand if you'd met my neighbor. Gray has nothing on that guy."

Tess waved her silent. "Emma, if you love Gray as much as you say and can't bear the idea of losing him, then marry him."

"I know he loves me as much as I love him. But..." Emma shook her head. "One half shouldn't be stronger than the other or the balance will be all wrong. One side ends up eclipsing the other. Before I commit to him, I have to know that he won't try to eclipse me."

"You don't think he can pull this off, do you?" Raine asked bluntly.

Emma crumpled the tissue she held. "No." She offered a shaky smile. "But I haven't lost all hope, yet."

CHAPTER TEN

Subject: Emma Palmer, Final Matchmaking Update
To: Committee@CupidCommittee.com
From: "Boss Lady"
<Adelaide@CupidCommittee.com>

At the risk of incurring our first matchmaking failure, I've decided to implement one final plan. Tee has been instructed what to do. If all goes as it should, Emma and Gray will be married by the end of the day.

Adelaide, President and CEO, Cupid Committee

GRAY stood in front of the church and fought to conceal his nervousness. Ruthless men weren't nervous. He was pretty sure it was an entrepreneurial law, and one of the more important ones, at that. One written in stone so it didn't get overlooked. If he were a betting man, which he was, he'd guess it ranked right up there with "take no prisoners" and "no holds barred."

That didn't change the fact that a bitter coldness had set in, infiltrating deep into his bones.

In an effort to distract himself, he examined the church with a calm, analytical eye. For a whirlwind wedding, all the various components had come together well. It was due in no small measure to half the town pitching in to give Emma the wedding of her dreams. Flowers overflowed the church, every possible variety present and accounted for. Knowing Emma, it was because she couldn't settle on any single type. But the florist had done an excellent job of combining the mixed array to stunning effect. White-satin ribbons covered every pillar and pew and an endless line of candles flickered with stately grandeur. He nodded in satisfaction. Not a hint of red or black, anywhere.

After what seemed like hours, the last of the guests took a seat and the music swelled. Gray gained a new appreciation for what his best friend had gone through two weeks earlier. No matter how badly he wanted to marry Emma, standing by himself in front of hundreds of curious onlookers was not his favorite way to spend a Saturday. And considering what was to come, his Saturday wouldn't be improving anytime soon.

With an intense feeling of *déjà vu*, Gray watched as the wedding party started up the aisle. Raine and Shadoe came first, followed by Tess and Shayde. Both appeared far too solemn for what should be a joyous occasion. Gray's brows drew together. Damn. They didn't think he was going to pull this off, either.

"Thanks for the support," he muttered when they came to stand next to him.

"What?" Shayde demanded. "What did we do wrong?"

"You look like you're at a funeral."

Shadoe grimaced. "Aren't we?"

"Not if I get this right," Gray replied.

"Any chance of that?" the two brothers asked in hopeful unison.

Gray fought to maintain an impassive expression. "I might surprise you, yet."

The flower girl and ring bearer approached the front

of the church. Unlike Tess's wedding they managed to
traverse the required distance without fighting and
without dumping flower petals all over the congregation. The ring bearer crossed to stand by Shayde.
Identical wedding bands—one large, one ridiculously
small—were tied to the white satin pillow the boy carried.

The organ music fell silent for a nerve-wracking instant before thundering out the opening strains of the
Wedding March, prompting everyone to rise. There
were too many people standing between Gray and
Emma and he couldn't see as she made her way up the
aisle with Tee. He fought the urge to shove everyone
into their seats so he could watch his bride come toward him. He suspected that might be a bit too ruthless,
even for him, though he was almost willing to risk it.
Finally she reached the front of the church and Gray
got his first good look at her.

He promptly forgot how to breathe.

She'd never been more beautiful. She wore her hair
up, pearls scattered like stars among the honey-colored
strands. A wisp of a veil cascaded down her back, pro-
viding a filmy backdrop to her wedding gown. The
dress was stunning, formfitting and elegant. The
dropped neckline framed her bare shoulders and a
slight bustle gave the gown a flirtatious appearance that
Gray found irresistible. Noticing his interest, she turned
slightly so he could see the back of her dress. A brazen
red bow rode the top of the bustle, flirting wickedly
with him with every twitch of her hips. He choked on
a laugh.

Tee released her arm and thumped his walking stick
against the carpet. "I want you all to know I'm not

happy about this,'' he announced in a booming voice. The organ music wheezed to a stop.

"Grandfather—" Emma began.

He cut her off without hesitation. "Don't grandfather me, girl. I came for a wedding and I have a nasty feeling I'm not going to get one." He glared at Gray. "And it's all your fault."

Gray nodded. "I'm well aware of that."

Tee transferred his glare to his granddaughter. "And what about you, missy? If you insist on going through with this nonsense, I expect you to be fair and reasonable." His ill humor assumed a calculating aspect. "Exactly how many guesses does the boy get for this second request of yours?"

The question prompted an instant reaction among the congregation. Quiet discussions broke out, rippling from front to back to front again. After a minute, the factory foreman spoke up. "I think he should get at least three. What do you say, Emma? Aren't three guesses traditional? Like in fairy tales?"

"That's wishes, you idiot," Tee retorted. "Though he's probably doing a hell of a lot of wishing right about now."

"I've been told we're not allowed to say 'hell' in church," Gray thought to mention. "At least, I'm not allowed to say hell, yes. And if I'm not allowed to say it, neither are you."

He was pointedly ignored.

"Three guesses," the foreman repeated, holding firm. "That's the consensus."

Murmurs of agreement met his stance.

"Okay, fine," Tee muttered. "Three it is. Personally I'd have given the boy a few more. Like a good round dozen. But if you only want three...."

Reverend Franklin glanced uncertainly at Emma. "How would you like to proceed? Should Gray tell you what he wants first, or do I start the ceremony?" He shook his head in clear disapproval. "I must say, this is all highly irregular. People are supposed to know whether they're getting married before they show up at the church. I'm not sure conditions and whatnots are allowed."

"Of course they're allowed," Tee argued. "That's why you ask the 'do you' questions. Gives them the opportunity to change their minds if they want. Sometimes they decide to go for the I do part and make their grandfather happy. Other times—" he scowled at Emma "—the I don't part holds foolish appeal."

Emma played with the bow decorating her bouquet as she considered. No one appeared at all surprised when it promptly unraveled, least of all Gray. Plucking it from her hands, he attempted to correct the problem, tying the silly thing in a double knot to make sure it held. It didn't look anywhere near as perky as it had before, but it would have to do. He was a ruthless entrepreneur, after all. And ruthless entrepreneurs didn't do perky. Or cute. Or even pretty. Expediency and positive results were his specialties. He gave the bow a final poke before handing it over.

Emma didn't seem to mind his lack of skill. But then, she never had. She accepted the bouquet with a warm smile of gratitude. "Thanks."

"You're welcome." Okay. Enough was enough. There wasn't any point in delaying further. Time to get the worst over and done with. "So, what's you're decision?" he prompted.

"I guess the requirements should come first before this goes any further." She looked up at him with such

a wealth of hope in her eyes, it was painful to witness.
"You're on."

"I was afraid you'd say that." He lifted an eyebrow.
"You sure you don't want to simply say hell, yes, and
be done with it?"

Emma released her breath in a disappointed sigh.
"You still don't have a clue, do you?"

"Quick!" Widow Bryant called out. "Tell her you
love her. Women always want to hear that."

"Not this woman," Emma denied without turning
around. She continued to gaze at Gray with bittersweet
tenderness. "I've always known he loves me. That was
never in doubt."

"And I do love you. More than words can express.
Never forget that."

Her mouth quivered ever so slightly, warning that
she wasn't quite as composed as she'd like everyone
to believe. He couldn't resist touching her. Gently he
swept a tousled lock of hair into place beneath her veil
and made a stab at levity—anything to erase the distress tainting the gold of her eyes.

"Does Widow Bryant's guess count as one of
mine?" he asked. "Because I don't remember agreeing
to a designated guesser."

"They're just trying to help."

Tee perked up at that. "That's right, sweetpea.
Everyone here's just trying to help." He turned to the
congregation, waggling his eyebrows in silent demand.
"Just *helping*."

It only took an instant for the townspeople to pick
up on his hint. "Kids!" someone shouted from a
nearby pew. "Maybe it's kids."

Tee groaned.

"It's not kids," Emma replied, adding wistfully, "Though I wouldn't mind a few."

Gray felt the need to interrupt again. "If my vote counts any—which remains in serious doubt—I'd like a passel. Passels have always appealed to me for some odd reason. There's something good and solid sounding about a passel."

Once again he was ignored.

"Diamonds," offered the florist. "Women love diamonds."

"Then how come you never buy me any?" his wife demanded.

Laughter broke out and Gray shook his head, half in amusement, half in disgust. "I guarantee, it's not something I can buy."

"A home. I'll bet she wants a real home. It's a nesting thing I've been told."

Tee shook his walking stick at the hapless man. "Use your head, you blithering idiot! It's not a home. Would he be standing here scratching his head if it were something easy like a home?"

"Besides, Gray's got a bunch of those already," Shayde added. "Not to mention that you can buy that, and we've already established that Emma isn't the sort of woman who can be bought."

"Maybe she wants him to move back to Palmersville. I'll bet living in San Francisco didn't agree with her. Too many strangers."

"Maybe she wants him to say he's sorry for taking over Palmer Shoes."

The factory foreman spoke up again. "Why should he be sorry about that? If it weren't for Gray we'd all be unemployed by now." He shot a guilty look in Tee's direction. "No offense."

"Offense taken," Tee snapped.

"Well, it's not like he got a good deal buying a controlling interest," the foreman retorted, sticking to his guns. "He must have sunk a fortune into saving the place. Probably his whole fortune."

Emma frowned. "Is that true?" she asked in an undertone.

Gray uttered a sound of annoyance. Hell. She wasn't supposed to find out about that. "Would it meet your condition if it is true?"

"I'm serious, Gray. Have you poured all your money into Palmer Shoes?"

"I'll see a good return. Eventually. Didn't Tee mention?" He folded his arms across his chest. "We're going into handmade designer shoes. All those deep pockets in Silicon Valley and San Francisco will be flocking to Palmersville to have us custom design everything from sports shoes to formal wear. We're already getting a decent number of orders."

"But until it's more than just a decent number?"

Gray shrugged. "I'm trained as an accountant, remember? I'm good at budgeting."

"Will you have to budget?" she persisted. "Will you have to budget because you rescued Palmer Shoes?"

He lifted an eyebrow. "So now I've rescued them? I thought I'd stolen the company from Tee."

"I'm serious, Gray."

"So am I." He regarded her with unwavering intensity. "Does it change our relationship if I saved the town by taking over Palmer Shoes?"

She sighed. "I bet I'm supposed to say no to that, aren't I?"

"You're damned right." He winced, catching himself an instant too late. "Sorry, Reverend."

The minister shook his head. "At this point, I'm not sure it matters anymore. We're probably all going to hell, regardless."

Gray returned his attention to Emma. "By rescuing Palmer Shoes I've suddenly become self-sacrificing and magnanimous. Is that it?"

She hesitated. "Okay. Maybe."

"Wrong."

"Darn it!" She smacked her bouquet against her thigh, decapitating a poor, helpless rose. "I knew that was the wrong answer. I should have said no. Right?"

"Right. You should have said no."

"But, *why?* Why isn't rescuing the factory self-sacrificing and magnanimous?"

Didn't she understand? "Because the only way I'm going to turn the company around and save the town is through sheer grit and ruthless determination. In this instance, ruthlessness is okay because everyone benefits. When it comes to you, though—" He shook his head. "It's a negative."

"There's a reason for that," she claimed.

"Time to end this, Emma. What's that old expression? A leopard can't change his spots? I'm sorry, honey, but I'm keeping my spots."

She stared in alarm. "What do you mean?"

"I love you." Sweeping aside her veil, he cupped her face and feathered a kiss across her mouth. Their lips clung for a brief, timeless moment. And then they parted. "I've loved you for more years than I can count. I want to marry you. I want to spend my life with you. To have children with you. To grow old with you. Either you love me and want those things, too, or you don't. But I'm not going to force you to marry me. And I'm sure as hell not going to ruthless you into it.''

''You're giving up?'' She grabbed hold of his wrists, refusing to let go. ''You can't. You're supposed to be too ruthless to give up, not so ruthless you walk away.''

He smiled, allowing himself a brief moment of amusement before growing serious once again. ''You were right, Emma. I don't know what your secret desire is. I thought I could figure it out. That I could approach the problem like I would a business situation. But obviously I can't.'' He freed himself from her hold and faced the congregation. ''End of the line, folks. No more guessing. All bets are off.''

There wasn't any point in continuing to stand there. He turned and headed down the aisle.

''Darn it, Gray!'' Emma started to throw her flowers to the carpet, thought better of it and tossed them to Tess, instead. Lifting the hem of her skirt, she charged after Gray, catching up with him halfway to the door. She grabbed the tails of his morning jacket and dragged him to a stop. ''You're not walking away from this.''

He spun around to confront her almost knocking her onto her backside. ''What's the point in staying? Don't you get it? I don't know what you want.'' He gestured to the congregation. ''They don't know, either.''

''Well, I do,'' Tee announced. He patted his pockets one after another until he located a cigar. Stripping off the cellophane, he clamped the unlit stogie between his back teeth. ''And you would, too, if you had just let me tell you. But, *noooo*. You had to be all noble and self-sacrificing instead of smart and conniving like I taught you. Mr. Ruthless, hah! Mr. Wuss, if you ask me.''

Emma swung around. "There's no way you could know what he's supposed to give me."

"Sure I do." Tee smiled in triumph. "I heard you tell your friends."

Emma's mouth fell open. "You heard—"

"Accidental, of course," he was quick to claim. "Did my best to pass the information on to the boy, but he wouldn't let me."

She switched her attention from her grandfather to Gray. "Is that true?"

Gray inclined his head. "Yes, it's true." Screw it. If he was going down, he'd go down all flags flying. "I'd already betrayed your confidence once. More than once if you want the truth. I was damned if I was going to do it again."

"What do you mean?"

"I mean that you were right. I am ruthless. And I'm not just ruthless when it comes to business. Hell, no. I take it into my personal life, too. In fact, I'm such a ruthless bastard that I contacted this group called the Cupid Committee who specializes in working behind-the-scenes to secretly match suitable couples. I asked them to do whatever it took in order to get you to marry me. I treated winning you like a business negotiation. I didn't care how they went about it, so long as the result was you in my bed, with my ring on your finger."

Tears pricked her eyes. "Gray—"

He cut her off. "I'm not finished. When Tee offered to tell me what your second request was, I almost accepted. I wasn't about to lose you over some ridiculous condition. After last night, I'd have done anything to give you what you wanted."

A faint color touched her cheeks at his mention of last night. "What stopped you?"

Gray's hands closed into fists. He'd always heard confession was good for the soul, but they would never prove it by him. Not unless torture could be described as something good. Because standing here, confessing his deepest feelings felt like sheer torture. "I couldn't bring myself to win by cheating, anymore than I could bring myself to lie to you about how I'd figured out your request. And I'd have had to lie, because knowing you, you'd have asked how I solved it."

"That's true enough." A hint of uncertainty invaded her expression. "That's all that stopped you from getting the information from Tee? You couldn't bring yourself to cheat?"

"Not quite." He dropped his hands onto her shoulders and pulled her close. She fit in his arms as though made for them. They belonged together. Couldn't she see that? "You looked at me funny."

"Excuse me?"

"In Tee's bedroom when we first got back from Seattle. You looked at me funny, like I'd hurt you somehow."

"That was because of Adelaide."

Gray stiffened. "Adelaide," he repeated.

"You didn't think I recognized her? Please." Emma shook her head in disgust. "Of course I did. I'm not a complete idiot. As soon as I saw her posing as my grandfather's nurse I suspected you and she had pressured Tee into making that deathbed demand of his."

"Like that old buzzard needed any pressure," Gray muttered.

"I guess that's why I looked at you oddly. I was disappointed that you'd try to trick me like that."

"Well, if it makes you feel any better, it's been driving me crazy these past two weeks. And it was enough to stop me from accepting insider information. Tee and I argued about it, and it was then that I finally understood what you'd been trying to tell me all this time. I've been turning my ruthlessness against you. And I realized that eventually it would destroy our love because I was attempting to run your life, instead of running with you." He released his breath in a gusty sigh. "Hell, honey. I'm sorry. I really am a Romulan. Right down to my DNA."

"You're wrong. Opposites have always been two halves of a whole," she whispered. "Neither one eclipsing the other."

"I suppose that's another way of looking at it." His brows drew together. "But why am I wrong? You said we were two alien species, and never the two shall mate. Why has that suddenly changed?"

"I'll tell you why," Tee crowed. "Because you did it. You actually figured it out all on your lonesome. Who'd have thought?"

Gray glared at Tee over the top of Emma's head. "What are you talking about, old man?"

Emma clung to him. "My second request." Her voice broke. "I wanted you to tell me that you'd gone to the Cupid Committee."

He pulled back so he could look at her. "You *knew* I went to them?" he asked in disbelief.

"Dammit, Tess!" Shayde growled. "You promised you wouldn't tell her."

Tess planted her hands on her hips. "Don't take that tone with me, Richard Shayde Smith. With all you Instigators ganging up on her, she deserved a fighting chance. And she sure wasn't going to get it if the Cupid

Committee stepped in." She grinned. "Personal experience taught me that much."

"How high-minded of you, my darling wife, considering you were the one who first approached us." Irritation rumbled through his voice. "You asked us to fix her up with Gray. Or have you conveniently forgotten that minor detail?"

Tess squirmed. "As a matter of fact, I had."

"How could you?" Emma protested. "You're supposed to be my friend."

"Hey, you asked me to find your soul mate if you weren't married by the time you turned thirty. So I did." Tess shook the bridal bouquet at her. "I was doing you a favor."

"Well, don't do me any favors," Raine broke in. "I remember that agreement. We were all of...what? Twenty? I'm officially retracting my part in it. I'm not interested in any sort of mate, soul or otherwise."

Tee stabbed his unlit cigar in the air. "My turn," he announced expansively. He rocked back on his heels, looking disgustedly pleased with himself. "I'm not normally a man who likes to admit to his misdeeds. Fact is, I quite enjoy getting away with the occasional transgression. But as long as we're confessin' our sins, I'm forced to admit I approached the Cupid Committee, too. Adelaide wasn't there at Gray's request. She was there at mine."

"Oh, dear. I suppose since everyone's confessing, so should I," Widow Bryant piped up. "In fact, my misdeed is even worse than all the others because I contacted the Cupid Committee on behalf of most of the town. There must have been near a hundred of us who decided to matchmake the two of you."

"Four requests?" Emma couldn't seem to take it in.

"Four of you approached the Cupid Committee on my behalf?"

"Now, honey," Gray began. "Don't get mad."

"Mad?" Tears gathered on her lashes and she broke into a wide, tremulous smile. "I think it's the sweetest thing anyone's ever done for me."

Gray shook his head. "There she goes taking a right turn when I expected her to go left."

"How about we all take a right turn and get this show on the road," Tee suggested. "Are we going to have a wedding or aren't we? I'm not getting any younger, you know."

"Well?" Gray asked Emma. "Will you marry me? No more requests, conditions or secret desires?"

She threw her arms around him. "Of course, I'll marry you."

Cheers greeted her response.

He tilted her face to his and waited for the noise to abate. "Why are you marrying me?"

She took the question in stride, no doubt realizing that he needed reassurance, too. "Because I love you. I love you for the man you are, not the man you think I want you to be."

He took a minute to unravel that. "You love me despite my being ruthless?"

"Yes." She smiled. "At least you're honest about it. And you did think with your heart. We'll just have to make sure that happens more often."

"I have to be honest, Emma. I'm not so sure I was actually thinking with my heart when Tee made his offer."

Tee nudged Reverend Franklin with his cane. "I suggest you get to the I dos while the getting's good," he suggested.

"Amen to that. Right here and now strikes me as best. And as short and sweet as possible." He fixed Gray with a stern eye. "Do you Grayson Earl Shaw take this woman for your lawfully wedded wife? Do you promise to love, honor, and never be ruthless toward her so long as you both shall live."

Gray kept his arms tight about his soon-to-be-wife. "I do."

Satisfied, the minister turned to Emma. "And do you, Emma Marie Palmer, take this man for your lawfully wedded husband? Do you promise to love, honor, and have no further conditions on your marriage?"

Emma grinned. "Hell, yes. I'll take this man."

Reverend Franklin wiped his brow. "Thank heaven. By the powers vested in me I now pronounce you husband and wife. This ends the betting pool. I've been advised by Mayor Hornsby that he'll be in the receiving line to pay off on all bets."

"The reception will have to wait," Emma informed her husband in an undertone.

He lifted an eyebrow. "And why's that?"

"We have more important matters to take care of."

"More important than our wedding reception?"

She nodded. "Much more important." She played with one of the onyx studs lining his dress shirt. It popped free and her hands shifted to the next one in line. "I want to get started on that passel of kids. Now, if you don't have any objections."

"Not a one." He didn't need any further prompting. Swinging her into his arms, he headed down the aisle. "Mayor Hornsby? The drinks are on me. You can use my share of the winnings from the betting pool. I won't need them. I've got all I want right here."

And he did.

The future looked bright and promising. Soon he'd have Palmer Shoes booming again. They would move permanently to Palmersville, and to a life among friends and family. In another few years, he and Emma would find themselves surrounded by that passel of kids they both wanted. The path leading to Nugget Creek would be used on a regular basis. And the tree fort would once again ring with young, happy voices. Sure, they'd have the occasional trouble with tribbles. But in the end, they'd live long and prosper. He'd see to that.

He'd make it so.

EPILOGUE

SHADOE poured champagne into a pair of crystal flutes and carried them to Adelaide's desk. "I have to hand it to you, boss lady. I didn't think we'd pull this one off."

His mother accepted one of the gently fizzing glasses. "We almost didn't," she replied. "That was a little too close for comfort."

"Damn right." He gave her a speculative look. "So what do you think? Has Gray learned his lesson?"

She grinned. "If he hasn't, I'm sure Emma will remind him."

"I don't doubt that for a minute." Taking the chair opposite her, Shadoe dropped a foot on the edge of her desk. "That just leaves Raine to match. It didn't sound to me like she was interested in our help."

"She isn't. So we'll treat this very delicately. One little nudge just to see what happens."

"Please tell me this one little nudge is going to be easier than the last two."

Adelaide shot him a pitying look. "Come now, Tom. After all these years, you should know better than that."

"I was afraid that's what you'd say." He took a long swallow of wine. "I assume you have someone in mind?"

"The perfect man," she confirmed.

"So who is it this time? Another capital of industry? Or is this one as ruthless as Gray?"

"I think this last match will come as quite a surprise to Raine." She offered her son a mysterious smile. "In fact, I'm willing to bet it's going to be an absolute bombshell."

Shadoe frowned. "What does that mean?"

"Sorry, sweetheart." She leaned across the desk and clinked her glass against his. "You're just going to have to wait until I'm good and ready to tell you. But I promise. You won't be disappointed."

Contract Brides

A wedding dilemma:
What should a sexy, successful bachelor do if he's too busy making millions to find a wife?

The perfect proposal:
The solution? For better, for worse, these grooms in a hurry have decided to sign, seal and deliver the ultimate marriage contract...to *buy* a bride!

Look out for these intensely emotional stories by some of our most popular authors, beginning with:

Susan Fox
MARRIAGE ON DEMAND
(April 2002, #3696)

Also look out for thrilling marriage stories by
Margaret Way
and
Leigh Michaels

Coming soon in
Harlequin
Romance®

HARLEQUIN®
Makes any time special®

HRCB

COOPER'S CORNER

The latest continuity from Harlequin
Books continues in October 2002 with

STRANGERS WHEN WE MEET
by Marisa Carroll

Check-in: Radio talk-show host Emma Hart thought Twin
Oaks was supposed to be a friendly inn, but fellow guest
Blake Weston sure was grumpy!

Checkout: When both Emma and Blake find their fiancés
cheating on them, they find themselves turning to one
another for support—and comforting hugs quickly turn to
passionate embraces....

HARLEQUIN®
Makes any time special ®

Possibly pregnant!

The possibility of parenthood: for some couples it's a seemingly impossible dream. For others, it's an unexpected surprise.... Or perhaps it's a planned pregnancy that brings a husband and wife closer together...or turns their marriage upside down?

One thing is for sure, life will never be the same when they find themselves having a baby...maybe!

This emotionally compelling miniseries from

Harlequin
Romance®

will warm your heart and bring a tear to your eye....

Look out in April for:
THE BABY QUESTION
by
Caroline Anderson
(#3697)

And keep an eye out for pregnancy stories by other popular authors such as:

Grace Green
Barbara Hannay

HARLEQUIN®
*M*akes any time special ®

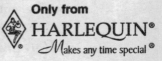